# THE SYSTEM OF VIENNA

OTHER WORKS BY GERT JONKE IN ENGLISH TRANSLATION

*Geometric Regional Novel*
*Homage to Czerny: Studies in Virtuoso Technique*
*Blinding Moment*

# THE SYSTEM OF VIENNA
## from heaven street to earth mound square

A novel by Gert Jonke
Translated and with an afterword by Vincent Kling

Dalkey Archive Press ⊑ Champaign and London

Originally published in German as *Himmelstraße—Erdbrustplatz oder Das System von Wien* by Residenz Verlag, 1999

Library of Congress Cataloging-in-Publication Data

Jonke, Gert, 1946-2009.
    [Himmelstrasse-Erdbrustplatz oder Das System von Wien. English]
    The system of Vienna, from Heaven Street to Earth Mound Square : a novel / by Gert Jonke
; translated and with an afterword by Vincent Kling.
        p. cm.
    "Originally published in German as Himmelstrasse-Erdbrustplatz oder Das System von
Wien by Residenz Verlag, 1999."
    ISBN 978-1-56478-550-3 (pbk. : acid-free paper)
    I. Kling, Vincent, 1942- II. Title.
    PT2670.O5H5613 2009
    833'.914--dc22
                    2009027584

Partially funded by a grant from the Illinois Arts Council, a state agency, and by the University of Illinois at Urbana-Champaign

The translator and publisher would like to thank the Austrian Federal Ministry of Education, Arts and Culture for financial assistance toward this translation

www.dalkeyarchive.com

Cover: design and composition by Danielle Dutton, illustration by Nicholas Motte
Printed on permanent/durable acid-free paper and bound in the United States of America

# CONTENTS

## AUTHOR'S NOTE ON PROVENANCE

For the most part, these Vienna stories correspond to a revised edition, by now long out of print, of my first stories, which appeared, in 1970 and 1980, respectively, under the titles "Music History" ("Musikgeschichte"), "Beginning of a Despondency" ("Beginn einer Verzweiflung"), and "The System of Vienna" ("Das System von Wien"). "Danube River Bridge" ("Reichsbrücke") was first published in 1980 on the album cover of André Heller's LP "Basta," "Caryatids and Atlantes" ("Karyatiden und Atlanten") that same year in the journal *manuskripte*. That short story, originally self-contained, was expanded into the framing plot of "Sleep War" ("Schlafkrieg").

—GERT JONKE

# BEGINNINGS IN A SMALL SOUTHERN AUSTRIAN CITY

Allow me first of all, in the interest of facilitating the greatest possible understanding, just a few brief words concerning the methodology of the working processes I have adopted, thereby also expending a few more words on myself and my academic development.

As you probably already know, I was born in a small provincial city in the winter of 1946, and some reference has been made to a few complications, albeit rather commonplace ones, in connection with my birth.

The story begins with a description of that cold winter night and how my mother allegedly started out not being able to find her shoes for a long time, locating them only after a frantic, extensive search and disappearing into the darkness of the February night after putting them on.

There follows the description of the trip—it struck her as endlessly long at the time—to a side entrance of the district hospital, which was actually located quite nearby, and the story of how she frantically rattled the locked door at that side entrance, slowly waking up the night porter, sound asleep, until he opened the window of his tiny porter's lodge and looked out scowling.

He's supposed to have explained to my mother that she wasn't permitted to enter the hospital by that door, but by the main entrance instead, because it wasn't the usual practice to enter the hospital by any of the side entrances, and moreover it wasn't even possible to open this particular one, whereas the main entrance, on the other hand, was open all night long, so she could certainly go in that way if she absolutely had to, but he couldn't open the door where they were, because after all he had strict instructions from the top, ones he was duty-bound to heed, just as there were specific strict instructions from the top for each and every one of us, and there was no such thing as refusing to comply with them, because why else would strict instructions like these exist if they weren't important, weren't essential to abide by them, and in every line of work there are rules and regulations that we all just have to make the best of, take for instance in his job as night porter, where he was under orders never under any circumstances to open this particular side entrance at night, no matter what might occur, and it didn't bear thinking what would happen if someone observed him opening it up, for there would be serious consequences, and he would be dismissed once and for all from his position as night porter, forever, and then he'd have to figure out how he, his wife, and his children could survive on air.

The story then tells how the porter turned a little gentler at the very last minute; there's something about a jangling search, about producing a bunch of keys, and finally about a raspy and then a screechy opening of the side door of the district hospital.

The ending has the night porter explaining how the mother was lucky he was there at all, because some consideration had been given shortly beforehand to reassigning him from the side door here to the main entrance, so that she would have been standing at a locked doorway and might then have had to go to the main entrance of the district hospital anyway, if she weren't to climb over the bars of the gateway, outfitted with iron spikes.

After that I—as the concluding expression goes—"turned up in no time," and, bringing the story to its end, there's a description of my skin, at that point completely blue.

# THE SMALL CITY ON THE LAKE

You know, I always make a connection between this small city, which I grew up in, and streetcars, even though no streetcars are in service there. Which leads to the conclusion that streetcars must have operated at one time, because how else would I ever have hit on the idea of connecting this place with streetcars?

Yes, there were streetcars traveling through this city at one time, from a train station to a cemetery, to be specific, and also, if I think really hard, to a lake shore, a landing dock, and the entrance to a swimming area with cabanas for changing and little bathing huts built of wooden planking which, at certain seasons of the year, mainly in autumn, emitted an extremely strong odor of tar.

If you go across the Alte Platz, or Old Square, you'll be blinded by the golden horns at the top of the Plague Memorial Column or by the Golden Goose, below which, coming out of the courtyard of the great Landhaus, the Renaissance estates building and now a museum, you will see hiding in the shadows of the Landhaus café the stag-beetle shapes of certain people, the kind known as shady characters. You continue, ambling past the artistically dazzling dances of the tongs and pliers in the display window of Zwick's hardware store, swimming through the lightning-bolt laughter of the work force at master electrician Senekovitch's place of business, while the yarns and woolen threads outstretched so helpfully toward you at Dörfler's haberdashery will indeed turn out to be very helpful to you as the owner scampers excitedly among his shelves trying to put down a revolt by buttons leaping out of their boxes; going past the mirrored display case showing the whole spectrum of colors at Hübner's paint store and the bolts of cloth at the fabric merchant Stuller's that billow out into artfully draped cloud-like shapes and stream out of the windows toward you with a rustling sound, you reach the fine-smelling soap bubbles foaming at regular intervals out of the walls at Leist's drugstore, sometimes achieving dimensions that make it possible for you, with no effort on your part, to find yourself enclosed in one of them and to float along, trapped inside, for quite a few yards, until it all becomes too much for you and you can't take any more, whereupon you simply wrap the Old Square up in thick brown paper with great care and neatly tie string around the package, which has ended up rather long.

When you've crossed over Bahnhof Strasse, where the station is, and go east on Priesterhaus Gasse, you'll come upon Getreide Gasse, proceeding north along which you could reach Rauscher Park with its statue erected to honor and commemorate the poet Rauscher, but you could of course keep following Priesterhaus Gasse to a square farther along, in the middle of which, honoring a certain long-departed Field Marshal Conrad, whom I never met personally, a roaring lion in slate has been placed, just behind which, though, continuing along a straight line, everything soon comes to a stop, because that's where, at the edge of the city, the metal storage huts begin where they keep the huge snow plows and storm equipment.

If you turn right, you'll soon be able to catch sight of the garden arrangements in Frick the scrap metal man's yard, in full bloom along with rusted kitchen ranges, ovens, and pipes, and then you'll come to the black gates of the wholesale vegetable dealer Valentin di Lenardo, behind which one of those famous masked galas of cabbages, cauliflowers, kohlrabis and all their kith and kin from the kitchen garden could very well be taking place right now.

Should you go in the other direction, however, you'll come after an uphill climb to another gate, this one belonging to Pagitz the fruit dealer, behind which a new Great Flood, this time of fruit juices, has long been in preparation, for which reason trucks are constantly driving into and back out of the courtyard, unloading wooden cases with empty bottles and reloading ones with bottles newly refilled.

You then make your way back downhill, past a tavern under the zodiac sign of the Hawke, and come once more to Bahnhof Strasse, where the sparkle from a gleaming tower instantly catches your eye; it's the Capuchin Church, enclosed by a black fence on which is mounted a showcase with the latest photographs of the Holy Father, the Holy Mother, the Holy Children, and most of the other kith and kin of the Holy Family.

Someone must have spread out the Old Square, which not long ago you had wrapped up in thick brown paper and tied very carefully with string, making it a longish package, because all of a sudden it's again become quite easy for you not only to cross it but also to let it sit just where it is, over your cold shoulder, once you're on the other side and then to launch and keep afloat on a raft of air, outward away from the city, the Lend Canal with its grass-weedscrubshrubovergrown banks, guiding it under and through several impeding bridges the jetties of which are floating or hanging athwart the direction you're moving in such that you'd be well advised to duck so as not to bump your forehead or your temples against the bars of the stair landings, along whose balustrades, in addition, a few anglers outfitted with fishing rods are quite likely to lean out and spit into the darkgreenblackcreepingplantalgaemurky water of this inland canal but at times, also, by that same action but with purely accidental intent, onto your crop of long blond hair as well, yes, yours, my lost love, perhaps yours, in spite of which you keep drifting farther and farther out from the city as the out-skirts continue flowing away, away from the mist hanging over the surprisingly short watercourse and onward, ever onward toward Lake Wörth (for how long now, by the way)—though what I'm do-ing with all this unchanneled talk of Lake Wörth I don't know, be-cause it might already have been the sea for quite some time now, for aren't those the endless coasts of an ocean whose shores have opened out to you, and are you now not once more so very far away that to you, here with me, this small city on the shore of an endlessly well-circumscribed but enormous vista facing us, its re-flection made up of patches of weather gathered from all the flat pieces of late-afternoon sky-horizon lying around until now, but now tossed into the bottom of the Klagenfurt Basin, as it's known, its whole surface framed by the interwoven hills lying in such meticulous juxtaposition throughout the area, swampy up to the knees when ventured into, but only at first, and then, much farther inside, around its midpoint, often sloping several hundred meters downward to the unexplored base of the quiet horizon it replicates, that horizon compassed with extraordinarily narrow margins but never actually crossed by so many glider-powered house boats, not one of which I could ever even begin to afford, let alone master the skill of navigating; very well, then, so is it not so that as far as you're concerned this small city and so much else besides—things that as far as I'm concerned might perhaps after all not quite so soon have been so entirely banished into oblivion (a process in which confidence can be reposed when any creature of habit is in question)—or, on the other hand and to an equal extent, is sunk in the pits and lagoons of your conscientiously clarified memory (so unfathomably deep that leaping forward with head thrust out would result in a smashed skull), that it's altogether as if one had not really been quite available to one's own self for a long time and the two parts have by now been constant in their search for one another throughout all the time that's passed by?

# CHILDHOOD IN THE COUNTRY

I spent the hot summers back in those years mostly at the house of a great-aunt in the country, though, where I would sink down into her garden as if into a subtropical rain forest, in the shadows of the larkspur along the trailers and stalks of vegetables with pods and hulls bursting open in the heat, planted all the way out to the twilit place where menacing stands of horsetail and hemlock woods lined a pondoceanswamp in the sour-smelling surf of which the afternoons coursed along, garbed as tribal migrations of dragonflies framed by a rainbow in a stream of light from all the wingèd crawfish in the sky, under whose evening attire my great-aunt would tell me about the most exciting and, to her, the most decisive moment of her life, which was what she referred to as the *Neumarkt air*, so good, so healthful.

Only once in her life, she was sorry to say, had she ever had an opportunity to breathe it, and very briefly at that, riding in a train that went through Neumarkt, which gave her the perfect opportunity to thrust her nose out of the window of the moving train.

However often she would put in a request to the local health officials for a period of rest and convalescence in Neumarkt, in theory fully covered, the people making the decisions never sent her there but always to some other place instead, which is how she had never had an opportunity to breathe the air of Neumarkt for longer than a few seconds, during that memorable train trip, that is, when she was able to stretch her nose out of the window of the moving train, having asked the conductor several times beforehand when they were coming to Neumarkt, so she wouldn't miss it. She could tell right away and was convinced on the spot: here was air like none other anywhere. Then she would describe that air by vigorously swinging her arms all around, thrashing about with them through the smoky air of the kitchen till the fortress walls of her sideboards would start splintering, her movements meant to demonstrate in the most graphic possible way how rich was the oxygen content in those lagoons of light that soared on high over the roofs of that village unknown to her yet and still.

In those days I often used to dream about my great-aunt at night. I would see her stretching her nose out of the window of the moving train, taking deep breaths as she inhaled the Neumarkt air through her nose, and then suddenly that nose would be squashed against a telegraph pole. She would fall backward in shock and only then, much too late, would she read the sign posted under the window that said Extending the nose out of the window when the train is en route through Neumarkt is prohibited!

And then, during the last summer I stayed with her in the country, I saw my great-aunt in a dream go floating through an open window of the train as it drove through Neumarkt, flying over the hills, powered by two gigantic wings of a nose that had grown out of her shoulder blades, beating the air as she fluttered away over the roofs of the village, soaring out past the crest of the Neumarkt hills and up into the mountains, toward the place where the streams of air had their source—all this in my dream, just before she suddenly died a few weeks later.

## OPERA SEMINAR—METTERNICH GASSE

I'm enrolled in a seminar called "Costumes and Their Dramaturgical Significance in Baroque Opera," and one day the professor asks me, of all people, if I might be willing to assist him at the Musical Academy while he delivers a slide lecture on Chinese and Indian theater, since he thinks I have the right kind of personality to insert and remove the slides from the projector.

During the seminar sessions he often talks about Chinese opera and Indian drama, even though the topic of the seminar doesn't have even the remotest connection to them.

He was in these Far Eastern countries for years, born in Indonesia, though of course not an Indonesian.

He's once more holding forth about Chinese actors, explaining methods of applying make-up in the Far East, the various costumes and their symbolic meanings, and why an actor will wear just one particular costume his whole life and never another. The actors, he emphasizes over and over, are bought from their parents when they're still children—yes, bought, all in due and proper order—and trained to be actors from the time they're small in the theater schools to which they're assigned.

While I'm thinking to myself that it's ridiculous for me to assist him, and I don't even want to anyway, though it's totally typical of me to do things I don't want to, I'm waiting for the professor at the Schottentor stop, as arranged, and sure enough, here he comes, and we ride together on the D trolley to Schwarzenberg Platz, then on the 71 to Metternich Gasse, and as we enter the opera department of the Musical Academy he draws my attention to the architecture of the mansion in which the academy is housed:

"This is how they built their homes toward the end of the last century; those nouveau riche who had conquered society in those days erected these mansions."

He leads me through the courtyard entrance, pointing out the elaborately wrought windows, interprets the meaning of all the stucco figures, the caryatids and atlantes along the walls, and leads me through the small theater auditorium to the rehearsal stage.

"We older people," he then comments, "grew up in this atmosphere, you know."

We use the bewildering, twisting system of staircases and corridors to climb to the highest floor of the building, set up the projector in one of the classrooms, and he fastens to the wall a piece of heavy white wrapping paper onto which the pictures are apparently going to be projected.

He bought the wrapping paper in a stationery store earlier, he said, because he knew there was no screen here in the opera department, which is why he bought the piece of wrapping paper earlier, he said, noticing during the purchase that the saleswoman in the store was unusually fat.

He can't find his slides; in fact, they're nowhere to be found, even though he carefully rummaged through his briefcase at least three times.

"I can't find my slides," he said, "and without my slides I can't give my lecture; it would be a disaster. I probably left them with the porter and then forgot. Of course I forgot; the porter must still have them. Would you mind going down to the porter and bringing back the slides?"

I go downstairs but can't find the porter.

I open all the doors, then I go back into the small theater with the rehearsal stage and ask someone where the porter is to be found.

The man shows me a small corridor along which I have to go.

I wanted to take this corridor even before I asked the man, but I thought it was a niche built deep into the wall.

I ask the porter—who, like all porters, is sitting behind a glass partition—about the slides the professor probably left with him and then forgot. The porter searches through his little glass dwelling but doesn't find anything.

I go back up, or rather try to go back up, but I can't find the classroom, so I go into the small theater, take a seat, then fall asleep while thinking, no, don't fall asleep.

While I'm trying to fall asleep a group of students enters the theater and takes occupancy of the rehearsal stage, which is when it occurs to me fully that I'm in the wrong place and should leave this room with utmost haste but instead run straight into the arms of the professor who's teaching that group of students, who's entered just behind them, looking at him with just as much amazement and astonishment as he's looking at me, until he finally asks:

"What's your business here? What exactly are you looking for? Whom are you trying to find?"

"I'm looking for the professor who's giving the illustrated lecture on Chinese and Indian theater," I answer.

He replies that he can't help me, knows nothing about any illustrated lecture being given anywhere in the building, and he's never even heard of Chinese or Indian theater, let alone seen any.

I continue wandering along various corridors and trying to fling open locked doors.

Sometimes I open the door of a classroom in which instruction is being given, and then I apologize for the disturbance.

Finally I ask someone where the classroom could possibly be located in which my professor is giving his illustrated lecture on Chinese and Indian theater.

The man points out a corridor I'd been meaning to follow several times already but hadn't, because I didn't grasp that it in fact was a corridor, thinking instead it was a niche carved deep into the wall.

I walk down it, eager to let the professor at last know he couldn't have left the slides with the porter after all, but the room is dark, all the lights out, too late, the lecture has already begun, and the professor is standing by the projector sliding the pictures through the machine himself.

I walk bent over so as not to cut across the beam of light the pictures are throwing onto the white paper mounted on the board, creeping along quietly, as quietly as possible so as not to disturb the lecturer's talk, and go up to him, then stand behind him and take over displaying the slides so as to give him a chance to concentrate entirely and exclusively on his presentation.

The illustrated lecture comes to an end; I apologize, explaining that I couldn't find the classroom again. The professor smiles and says that's all right, these things happen, in fact they've happened to lots of people; then he thanks me, says it was very nice of me to have helped him, in fact I was a great help, and little mishaps like these aren't even worth mentioning.

He takes me along with him in a cab, and as we're riding through Schwarzenberg Platz, that broad square, he points out the French Embassy.

"Doesn't it strike you as very strange that this building should be standing exactly where it's in fact situated?" he asks me.

"No," I answer.

"Don't you notice anything about the building?" he follows up.

"No."

"You really don't notice anything peculiar about it?"

"I couldn't tell you what's so peculiar that I should be noticing."

"Well, do you think this building could just as well be standing somewhere else?"

"I don't know," I say.

"Didn't it ever occur to you that this building is standing in the wrong place, was constructed on the wrong spot?"

"No."

"Take a look, though. Don't you see that the building shouldn't be standing where it is? The French Embassy over there was built in the wrong place, although no one intended it to be, but they delivered the wrong plans to the construction firm; they sent to the construction firm in charge of the French Embassy in Vienna the plans for the French Embassy in Bangkok, and delivered to the construction firm in charge of building the French Embassy in Bangkok the plans for the French Embassy in Vienna. They simply switched the sets of plans, so the building housing the French Embassy which should have been built in Vienna is now standing in Bangkok, while the building housing the French Embassy that should have been standing in Bangkok is here in Vienna, over there where you can look at it any time! So that's what we wind up with right here on Schwarzenberg Platz!"

## FURNITURE SHOW—MAIN PROMENADE IN THE PRATER

One hot day I went to a trade fair and show sponsored by Vienna's furniture manufacturers. I went to the show only because somebody had told me that the furniture was going to be set up not in the display areas and showrooms but out in the open, on the grounds around the exhibition hall. The main reason I went to the show in the first place was because I didn't want to miss the sight of all those wardrobes, kitchen sideboards, night stands, beds, etc., standing out on open ground, and if someone hadn't told me about it being out in the open, I would never have gone to the show, since furniture does not interest me now, never has interested me, and never will interest me.

As soon as I stepped inside the pavilion where the show was being held, a gentleman dressed in black, who stepped away from a whole crowd of men congregating in a corner and likewise all dressed in black, came up and spoke to me. "It is an unusually great honor for me as the personal representative of the Chancellor, who is unfortunately prevented from attending in person, to extend a warm welcome to you as the hundred thousandth visitor to the Vienna Furniture Show."

He shook my hand vigorously and then pressed a book into that same hand. Title of the book: *The System of Vienna.*

The other twenty or thirty gentlemen dressed in black then came up to me one by one, a twenty- or thirty-fold handshake then ensued, and each of the twenty or thirty gentlemen dressed in black asked me what I did for a living, how I was, how I occupied myself, and I explained in turn to each of these twenty or thirty gentlemen dressed in black that they were speaking with a musicologist.

After that the personal representative or confidant of the Chancellor took me aside and whispered in a questioning tone, "May I treat you to a mug of beer?" and I answered, "Most certainly you may."

I went with him then into a nearby tavern, we took seats, and he ordered two mugs of beer. Then suddenly he whispered, "You know, sometimes it strikes me as odd that I'm the Chancellor's confidant, I mean me of all people, and sometimes I think I'm not the Chancellor's confidant at all—a regrettable mistake—and someone completely different is in reality the Chancellor's confidant." And sometimes, the Chancellor's confidant said, the Chancellor feels exactly the same way as he, his confidant, does. "The Chancellor said to me once," the confidant said, "how odd it strikes him sometimes that he of all people is the Chancellor," and sometimes he, the Chancellor, thought, as he told his confidant, that he wasn't the Chancellor at all, a regrettable mistake that he's the Chancellor, and in reality somebody completely different is probably the Chancellor. But then, the Chancellor's confidant said, the Chancellor all of a sudden pulls himself together and says to him, his confidant, that of course it's perfectly obvious that he, the Chancellor, is the Chancellor, and how could it ever even cross his, the Chancellor's, mind that he isn't the Chancellor?

The Chancellor's confidant ordered two more mugs of beer, but then all of a sudden started up with alarm and asked, "How could it have come about just now that I told you how odd it strikes me that I'm the Chancellor's confidant, how I sometimes believe I'm not the Chancellor's confidant at all, even though I am indeed the Chancellor's confidant?" The Chancellor's confidant then said that of course he's the Chancellor's confidant, so how could it ever even cross his mind that he wasn't the Chancellor's confidant?

I believe the Chancellor's confidant was trying in the words that followed to discover a cause for the turn his conversation with me had taken at this season, its heat sending everyone's head hurtling through the firmament.

Bringing our conversation here in this tavern to an end, the Chancellor's confidant mentioned the Chancellor once again, telling me that the Chancellor, after a few more successful years as the Chancellor, would in all probability accept a chair at the university.

As we left the tavern, I said good-bye to the Chancellor's confidant and thanked him for the beer.

Now I wanted to get away from the area around the furniture show immediately, because I had not seen anything of the furniture supposedly being displayed on the grounds around the exhibition hall, and the furniture being displayed inside the exhibition hall did not interest me; furniture had never interested me in the least. But then several of the gentlemen dressed in black, who were still standing around the entrance to the area where the furniture show was being held, asked me if I wouldn't like to come in and have a look at the furniture show. I thereupon explained quite bluntly to the twenty or thirty gentlemen dressed in black that I hadn't come here for the furniture show and in fact never went to furniture shows; for that matter, going to furniture shows is just not something I do; instead, I had come only because someone had told me the furniture would be on display not in the showrooms and pavilions of the exhibition hall but out on the grounds around the exhibition building, and the sight of furniture standing out in the open was what had induced me to come to this furniture show, since I had never seen furniture standing out in the open, whereas furniture in rooms, especially in display rooms of exhibition halls, did not interest me.

Then I really did leave the area around the furniture show immediately. The book the Chancellor's confidant had handed to me I set down in the nearest wastebasket. It was a very hot day, and I felt it would be too bothersome, uncomfortable, and pointless to carry a book under my arm. Title of the book: *The System of Vienna.*

## AUTUMN MIST—ROSE HILL

One day I boarded the city train at the Gürtel, the Outer Beltway, rode to Hietzing, then at Hietzing Bridge took the 60 streetcar going out to Rodaun but got off at the Rose Hill-Riedel Gasse stop, then walked along Riedel Gasse, past all the fencing that separates the grounds of the psychiatric hospital from the street.

I have only a vague memory of the high fences, the covering of snow, the houses and villas lining the street, and a building site, where a worker was erecting some wooden scaffolding.

It disturbed me that this workman had nailed in all the planks horizontal from the ground up, so I went over to him and asked beseechingly, "Won't you set this plank in vertical to the rest? Don't you see it's supposed to be like that?"

All he did was give me a stupid look and then nail that plank, as well as all the ones after it, parallel to all the others while looking at me in a puzzled way as I started back down the street, which is probably what I did.

You can sense it; if someone's looking at you, you can sense it, even when your back's turned.

I must have come to the top of a hill; a patch of dark woods was erected in front of me.

I remember having seen each district of Vienna, how on days like this they lie outspread in the mist, how on such days you think life is following catacomb-like pathways below the surface of the street.

Then I saw the sculptor, how he had set up a plaster sculpture under a tree; I went up to him and stood beside him.

"Do you like it?" the sculptor asked, and for the sake of politeness I said yes.

I no longer remember what the figure was like that he'd shaped; I only know that I felt it, as a representation of the gray autumn air transferred into some solid material substance, to be every bit as unpleasant as these misty, foggy days, on which everything seems to have been shrouded away and sent veering off.

I bet you believe I'm a sculptor, the sculptor said, but that's a mistake.

You believe I'm standing here under this tree and busying myself with this admittedly unusual sculpture, but that is not at all how things are, no, and that you are now standing here beside me is also purely a matter of your imagination, just as it goes without saying that we're always quite naturally located somewhere other than circumstances would make it appear, so listen carefully, for in all probability we are located in no place other, oh yes indeed, than in a—how do you say it—more or less enclosed space, a room that has a suspiciously familiar appearance to us, you won't think it's possible, but what are we doing here after all, well now you won't even believe it, but listen carefully, for we're sitting, yes, sitting at a table, in all probability at a table, and what is it we're doing, oh you'll be amazed, because what we're doing is writing, oh yes indeed, we're writing, and what we're writing to begin with is that we're—how do you say it—sitting, yes sitting in this room, but that alone won't be enough for us, you understand, for since when is it enough just to be writing

something, just simply to write that we're sitting in a room suspiciously closed in on itself, no, so let's write something different,
let's not write that we're not sitting in this room, no; so what will
we write instead, oh you won't be the least bit amazed, yes indeed,
you'll understand enough to have insight into how we can write anything whatever, just not anything about this room, and while you're
writing that you boarded the city train at the Outer Beltway, rode to
Hietzing, then took the 60 streetcar going out to Rodaun but got off at
the Rose Hill-Riedel Gasse stop, next went past the psychiatric hospital and came to a building site, oh yes, listen carefully, while you've
been writing that you watched a workman at this building site as he
erected some wooden scaffolding by nailing the planks according to
a very specific plan of construction, the structure of which did not
fit in with your ideas on the matter, which, however, you will have to
concede without insisting on your own way, can hardly be the fault
of the workman, having been in all probability much more the fault
of deficiencies arising from your unclear manner of writing and ex-
pressing yourself, in turn ascribable to deficiencies in your technique
of depicting objects (you really must express yourself more clearly in
the future so as to avoid such conflicts with the working class)—so
while you were writing, or rather during your presentation using as
an excuse that you had no other choice but to make the workman
all confused and thus—with malice aforethought, it would almost
seem—to cause him to become upset, albeit that effort, owing to your
manner of expression, did not entirely succeed (now listen carefully,
in future you will have to make your point somewhat more clearly so
as to avoid this kind of conflict with members of the proletariat; such
quarrels with people who do heavy labor can eventuate in greater
difficulties than would arise from an uncomprehending shake of the
head); now yes indeed, while you've been writing that you continued

up the street, reached the top of this hill, and observed from above the city you described, and I emphasize the city you described, and then wrote further that you suddenly caught sight of me, yes indeed, of me with a sculpture of mine, one described first by me and then by you, and then went on to write, yes indeed, that you came and stood beside me, I was all the while making matters considerably simpler for myself and describing them simply, how I'm standing under this tree waiting for you and busying myself pending your eventual appearance on the scene with an alleged sculpture, as such a thing is called, you understand, one which to you and me as well can be understood if we think of it as a representation, shaped and transferred into some solid material, of the gray autumn air in the mist and fog of this day, a day on which you think life is following catacomb-like pathways below the surface of the street.

I spent what could well have been the whole rest of that day standing at the streetcar stop, just standing there until far into the night. As if I were going to keep on waiting beyond even the break of gray dawn for a 60 that would never again come. It kept pulling up and driving past me, however, very frequently, exactly on schedule, and with ever greater persistence, but increasingly and with ever greater persistence, quite deliberately and purposely, not taken note of by me, starting while it was still a good distance away. Even the personal invitations of many different streetcar conductors finally to please board were altogether fruitless.

I have presented my physical person more and more clearly as an image of someone seized for the rest of that day by a kind of "vertical" winter sleep.

The one thing I do remember, however, is that house next to the streetcar stop and a woman who the whole time, without interruption, kept on shaking dust cloths and cleaning rags out of one of the windows. Over and over and over again. Until far into the night.

I believe even far ahead of and well into the breaking dawn of morning gray at that!

# THE STAMP COLLECTOR IN THE VIENNA WOODS

I'm taking a walk through the Vienna Woods.

I hear the call of a tawny owl.

Since it's not usual to hear an owl during the day—we're talking about a typical night bird—I'm very surprised.

While I'm thinking this whole thing over, a man wearing a black coat and a bowler hat jumps out from behind a rock face, lifts his hat, and says good afternoon. Good afternoon, I answer.

I'm almost sure it wasn't the tawny owl but rather this man with the black coat and the bowler who produced the call of the night bird; yes, the man with coat and bowler hat could have imitated the cry of the tawny owl; I realize right away, in fact, that I wouldn't put it past him.

Naturally I feel he's making fun of me, but the man probably wasn't trying to make fun of me or put something over on me at all; it's quite possible, I think, that the man with the bowler hat and the black coat was mimicking by day the voice of a night bird strictly for his own amusement just as I happened to come along.

Because I took him by surprise, he might have thought he had no other course of action than to jump out from behind the rock and acknowledge me. What I could have taken him by surprise doing is a mystery to me.

He walks up to me and extends his hand.

He probably has the feeling—and he's completely right if he has—that he could appear to be a comical character in my eyes.

The man might well be harboring the suspicion that in my eyes he's a ridiculous individual, which is in keeping with the fact, for that matter, but no one wants to be ridiculous or a figure of fun; everyone wants to be taken seriously, and so now he wants to prove that he can cut a figure as a person to be taken seriously.

That is to say, he wants to rehabilitate himself in my eyes.

Zett is my name, he says, but if you don't happen to remember the name "Zett," you may call me by my first name.

Zett then asks if he may walk a short way with me, because we're going in the same direction.

Yes, he may.

But how and why does he know enough about what direction I'm going in to decide it as being the same as his own?

If you have any trouble remembering or pronouncing my last name, please feel free to call me by my first name, as I said, because even though my name would appear to be easy to remember and pronounce, the opposite has usually turned out to be the case; incidentally, you can't give the City of Vienna enough credit for having left this area in a state of nature and not allowed any development; yet it's exactly areas like these that are exceptionally dangerous, because in these isolated surroundings, beautiful enough that they simulate a frivolously cosmetic image of the state of the world, which as a consequence misleads us into abandoning ourselves with such great verve to primped-up landscape lies like these that we slip so far away from our own vision, our very own eyes, as to grow incapable of locating the lost objects of our searches during ever more urgent searches for our objects, the upshot of which is that we, by being the seeker as well as the sought, at no time and in no place ever find a way back to ourselves because of an *utter entanglement* that keeps multiplying itself over and over in constant mutual duplication.

Suddenly a few of those tame wild pigs like the ones that have the run of the Lainz Zoo by the hundreds came up to us and rubbed their dark grey backs against his long black coat till he pulled several pieces of bread out of his coat pocket and tossed them into their snouts, whereupon the wild pigs went scampering away.

There you are, stated Herr Zett, you could only have such an experience in undeveloped surroundings like these, left as nature shaped them. He spends a long time listening to the whooshing and rustling of branches and other noises made by the wild pigs as they scuttle away.

I'm actually a philatelist, that is, a passionate stamp collector, he continues, trying to expound to me all the good points about stamp collecting.

What I demand on behalf of my passion is that it should be categorized not just as a passion, but also as a science, a branch of scholarship. I consider philatelistics an area of research which still today should be accorded utmost seriousness, since the other sciences, whether they're called mathematics or physics, have obviously lost whatever meaning they once had.

Anyone who believes that science and scholarship are actually being pursued in the scholarly and scientific departments of the universities is laboring under a regrettable mistake. If a man is wearing twenty pairs of pants, everyone who encounters him believes he's wearing not twenty pairs of pants but a single pair of wide-flared knickerbockers. Everyone ought to be able to recognize right away that the thinking at our universities is more a *knickerbocker way of thinking*. But even a person who comes to realize that is in danger of laboring under an additional regrettable mistake. Specifically, the people at our universities are not wearing knickerbockers at all, but it's easy to think they are, because it looks altogether as if they were indeed wearing knickerbockers, whereas in reality they have *twenty pairs of pants* on: twenty torn pairs of pants. That is why scholarship as engaged in at these institutions is not even knickerbocker scholarship but merely *twenty-pairs-of-pants scholarship*. It would be very nice if the scholarship being pursued there were knickerbocker scholarship, at least, but it's merely a pathetic example of *twenty-pairs-of-pants-university-style scholarship*, and the thinking in the departments at our universities is nowhere near being knickerbocker thinking, sad to say; it's *twenty-pairs-of pants thinking* instead. Mostly, however, the people involved in their scholarship at these institutions are wearing not twenty pairs of pants, but none at all. That is why the scholarship as pursued at our universities is not even twenty-pairs-of-pants scholarship, but instead no scholarship at all, and the thinking at our universities isn't even so much as twenty-pairs-of-pants thinking, but an unimaginable chain of utter mindlessnesses instead. That state of affairs is for the most part very well known, even at our universities, which is why the people who there engage in what they term scholarship are now attempting at least to disguise the scholarship they term scholarship—though it does not even represent knickerbocker scholarship—as twenty-pairs-of-pants scholarship.

So what they're pursuing is a kind of *sham knickerbocker scholarship* or *sham twenty-pairs-of-pants-scholarship* while really fooling themselves by their own *sham knickerbocker thinking* and *sham twenty-pairs-of-pants thinking.*

While all the other branches of scholarship are sinking to lower and lower levels, the level of philatelistics is noticeably rising; I am using the word "philatelistics" on purpose, because as of yet there is no suitable expression for the concept, and the designation "stamp collecting" would reduce that branch of scholarship to the status of a mere agreeable hobby.

Have I ever given any thought, Herr Zett asks, to the question of what the difference between the Yugoslavian postage stamp with the head of Yugoslavian King Alexander before his death and the Yugoslavian postage stamp with the head of Yugoslavian King Alexander immediately after his death consists of?

No, I answer.

Ah, you see, Herr Zett explains, the stamp with the head of King Alexander before his demise has a white border, and the stamp with the head of King Alexander immediately after his demise has a black border.

Then the stamp collector proceeds to draw my attention to the significance of nature and animal series and assures me that in Austria a whole series of wild pigs is going to be issued in the near future; reproductions of wild pigs on red, yellow, black, blue, brown, and violet backgrounds.

What you should know, the stamp collector explains further, is that I am the president of the Austrian Philatelistic Society and at the upcoming Philatelistic Conference will in all probability be elected president of the European Philatelistic Society, because the current president of the European Philatelistic Society intends to retire, and so if you should happen to hear about a professorship in the area of philatelistics being vacant, please keep me in mind, because my aim is to teach *systematic and general philatelistics* and the *history of philatelistics* as well.

I should pay a visit to the Philatelistic Society some time, he says, should listen to one of his lectures; all I need to do is call the Philatelistic Society, whose number I can find in any telephone book, mention the name *Zett* just once, then say—here's what I should say—I'm calling because Herr Zett suggested I should call, and once they hear the name Zett they'll be forthcoming with any and all information I could ever want, for as soon as I drop his name, there's simply nothing that can go wrong.

It was a good long time after Herr Zett had said good-bye to me that I realized I'd forgotten the most important thing of all, which was to ask him whether it was he who had imitated the call of the tawny owl earlier or whether it really was a tawny owl.

# WHOLESALE FISH DEALER BY THE DANUBE CANAL

On clear spring evenings I've often taken walks up and down the banks of the Danube Canal.

I'll mention the air that rises up from the Danube Canal, the palatial insurance headquarters and their lighted advertising signs reflected in the water. Also the arches of the lighted or black bridges, repeated in the water in inverse proportion, and I'll talk about stone walls and bricks along the bank. And I'll talk as well about a wholesale fish market, how it reminds me of the sea, and the fishvendors' huts along the bank.

On one of those mild spring evenings I walked past one of those fish wholesaler's huts and observed a fish wholesaler, who had just closed the metal gate of his fish wholesaler's hut.

I walked by him just as he was about to finish closing the iron door behind him. Right after that he let out with an exceedingly loud "finally." It was at the very moment of this exceedingly loud "finally" that I went walking past him and could not refrain from giving expression to my astonishment by glancing his way with what I can only suppose was a very strange look.

This astonished look on my part must have been what induced him to speak to me; there are quite a few people, after all, who will strike up a conversation if someone has for any reason looked at them strangely—or for that matter not the least bit strangely.

"Maybe you have some idea!" he said. "Maybe you have some idea! When you spend the entire day in the company of fish, in the company of fish you're weighing, have to weigh; when you have to spend the entire day giving people orders to weigh fish."

He took me off to the side and said: "Come, I'll unlock this door; for your sake I'll unlock this door once more."

He felt in his pants pocket for the key, his small, stocky body bent over on a slant, and all the time that his hand was rummaging around in his pants pocket he was having trouble finding the key, but he finally moved his overcoat aside and then found his bunch of keys in a pocket under his ash-colored coat.

Then he hunched down so he could reach the keyhole, which was only ten centimeters above the ground, put the key into the keyhole, turned it, and slid the gate up.

Then he took me into his fish wholesaler's hut and said: "What if you had to spend the entire day here in the company of these dead fish!"

What astounded me, however, and to the greatest extent imaginable, was not seeing one single fish, no matter how long and how hard I looked around, not one single fish in this wholesale fish-dealer's place of business, out of whose walls wooden boards, planed and smoothed like table tops, had "grown" at chest height.

I didn't see one single fish, although based on the odor around the place I had constantly been expecting to encounter fish, dead fish.

It's possible, though, that these fish I was conjecturing might have been put away in wall cabinets not within my sight.

"I bet you believe," he started by saying, "that I'm a wholesale dealer in fish, but that's a far-reaching mistake!" In reality he wasn't a wholesale fish dealer at all; it just looked as if he were a wholesale fish dealer, and it would be altogether legitimate to believe on a continuing basis that that's what he was; all the better, in fact, he said, for people to believe on a continuing basis that he's a wholesale fish dealer; you could never overestimate how valuable it is that people believe he's a wholesale fish dealer or how useful it could prove. In reality, though, he wasn't a wholesale fish dealer at all, having entirely different interests from those pertaining to wholesale fish dealing, his existence as a fish wholesaler being no more than a method of covering up the truth, and a truly outstanding one at that. In reality, he said, taking me secretively off to the side, in reality he, whom everybody thought of as a wholesale fish dealer, wasn't a fish wholesaler at all; no, he said, he wasn't a wholesale fish dealer, but a *political figure* instead!

"If you believe," he said, "that politics are run by those people who call themselves political figures, then you have fallen victim to a serious mistake! Because for those who call themselves political figures, being in charge of politics represents a mere deception, a tremendous cover-up perpetrated on the public. Those people call themselves political figures but in reality are no such thing; they only want to convince all the people that that's what they are, whereas they are no such thing," just as he, the fish wholesaler, wanted to convince all the people that he was a wholesale fish dealer, while in reality he was no such thing, being none other than a political figure instead. "It's entirely possible," he went on to explain, "that the political figures who are called political figures are in reality tailors, vintners, handymen, carpenters, teachers of special education, bricklayers, health-care workers, or butchers," just as he, the fish wholesaler, was not a wholesale fish dealer at all, but a political figure instead. And just as those people who call themselves political figures consider to be a good thing the general assumption that they are political figures, whereas they're no such thing, but grocers or railroad inspectors instead, so he, too, the fish wholesaler, considers the general assumption that he is a wholesale fish dealer to be a good thing, whereas he's no such thing, but a political figure instead.

"You never know how useful that might prove," he went on to explain; "politics are never controlled by political figures, just as wholesale fish dealing is never engaged in by fish wholesalers. Politics are in the hands of people one would never even surmise were political figures. Many people say politics are the domain of what are called lodges or intellectual, highly intellectual organizations or associations. But in reality even those very lodges, as they're called, or those intellectual, highly intellectual organizations or associations exist for the purpose of offering an opportunity to provide various groups the possibility for maintaining that they, the lodges, actually control politics and make all the decisions."

"The real politics are managed by people no one would ever even dare to categorize as political figures." And he himself was a kind of intellectual leader of those people who actually controlled politics and decided everything that was going to happen. He was the intellectual leader of those people, he, the wholesale fish dealer, of whom it was asserted that he was this particular fish wholesaler by the Danube Canal.

He said: "Practically everyone will assert that the Chancellor is the head of government; that's a mistake, of course, because the

Chancellor has the party ideologue behind him; the Chancellor is nothing but a puppet of the party ideologue and must carry out all the orders given by the party ideologue. Only a select few know that. So now you'll think the party ideologue is the real head of government, since it is he, the party ideologue, who gives the Chancellor his orders, but that too is a mistake, because the party ideologue has his secretary behind him; the party ideologue is nothing but a puppet of his secretary and has to carry out all the orders given by his secretary; the party ideologue must pass on to the Chancellor whatever orders his secretary gives him." The Chancellor then believes that the orders that the orders given by the party ideologue came out of his own, that is the party ideologue's, head, but the Chancellor is mistaken, because those orders did not originate with the person of the party ideologue but have as their source the secretary of the party ideologue instead.

"Now," the fish wholesaler continued to expound, "you will think the secretary of the party ideologue is the real head of government, since he's the one giving the orders to the party ideologue, who then communicates them to the Chancellor. But that's the strangest mistake about this whole business," because, the fish wholesaler explicitly stated, standing behind the secretary of the party ideologue was he, the wholesale fish dealer himself, yes, he, the fish wholesaler stands behind the secretary of the party ideologue, he, the wholesale fish dealer, of whom everyone believed he was this fish wholesaler by the Danube Canal, and the secretary of the party ideologue was merely his puppet and had to carry out his orders, conveying them to the party ideologue, who then had to pass them on to the Chancellor. "The party ideologue," the fish wholesaler continued, "believes the whole time that the orders reaching him come out of his secretary's head, just as the Chancellor believes that these orders come out of the party ideologue's head, but that's a mistake, because the orders given by the party ideologue no more come out of the party ideologue's head than the orders given by the secretary of the party ideologue come out of the head of the secretary of the party ideologue; instead, all the *orders come out of my head!*" And if anyone then thinks that he, the wholesale fish dealer, is the real head of government, then that person isn't so completely wrong; in fact, that person is fully and accurately informed as to the actual circumstances and facts of the matter, for he, the fish wholesaler, is indeed the real head of government, since the Chancellor—albeit in roundabout ways—is nothing more than his puppet, and so the Chancellor is required to carry out all the fish-wholesaler orders conveyed to him, the Chancellor, via these roundabout ways, of whose very existence the Chancellor has not even the faintest idea. "So as you see," the wholesale fish dealer said, "I'm the real Chancellor, because everything proceeds and is carried out according to my decisions."

These roundabout ways of communicating orders and passing on instructions have severe disadvantages, however. The wholesale fish dealer began speaking about all the unnecessary waste of energy. "These roundabout ways of communicating orders and these intricacies in passing on instructions, because they are often so extremely complicated, do not always proceed without friction; on the contrary, their execution produces great friction, and through constant friction energy is lost, and when it comes to friction, the energy is lost as heat that can no longer be put to use; my orders and instructions lose energy!" Too much command energy is wasted; no usable instruction energy is left.

Therein was to be sought the reason and the cause why things are sometimes, mostly sometimes, rather often, sometimes rather often, mostly sometimes rather often, mostly rather often, sometimes mostly mostly, mostly mostly not as they should be.

"Because too much command energy goes to waste." That is why there will some day be no way out other than to issue to the secretary of the party ideologue an order to the effect that he is required forthwith to move forth with the action of taking the Chancellor's place, because things just cannot keep going on the same way, so nothing else will do but finally to install a chancellor as head of government who is not a puppet. The secretary of the party ideologue will then pass on the order to the party ideologue, who will deliver it to the Chancellor.

The fish wholesaler suddenly burst out into uproarious laughter, laughing so hard he even had to catch his breath, and continued in a gloating tone, his laughter at times making him slur his words: "Right at the start the Chancellor will be amazed, because he doesn't have the faintest inkling that I, a wholesale fish dealer by the Danube Canal, even exist; he will in all probability attempt to refuse the order, because he surely could not have any intention, at least not yet, of giving up his office, but in the end no other course of action will be left to him than to step down, since he is nothing but a puppet of the party ideologue, the party ideologue nothing but a puppet of his secretary and the secretary of the party ideologue nothing but a puppet of mine!"

Returning from his momentary and almost passionate outburst of hilarity to a certain degree of businesslike demeanor, the fish wholesaler then went on to explain that it would take a long time for this latter order to be carried out, because, as a result of complex methods of communicating orders and passing on instructions, ones he had not long previously given me an account of, a great deal of command energy would go to waste, thus becoming unusable; it was entirely possible, for that matter, that the order to change Chancellors would cause so much energy to be wasted that he would have to repeat it a second, fourth, eighth, tenth, fiftieth, hundredth time. "But sooner or later will be taken due note of, the Chancellor will step down, I will assume his duties, and no one will think there's anything the least bit peculiar about it; I will be a true Chancellor and not a puppet!" Then he would play an altogether different tune, he said. "Altogether different!"

For the time being, however, he was still the fish wholesaler, the wholesale fish dealer, whom everybody thought of as a fish wholesaler, which in reality he was no such thing as, though it's all to the good for people everywhere to believe that's what he is, and you never knew in how many ways that could prove useful. Then he said, he might just as well close up the fish wholesale store now, because he had shown me in detail his wholesale fish dealership, in which I had not seen one single fish, even though the smell of dead fish was practically turning my stomach. The fish dealer used one of his hands to move aside his overcoat, then took a key out of one of his pants pockets, lowered the metal gate of the wholesale fish store, bent down, put the key into the keyhole (ten centimeters above the ground) of his fish wholesaler's gate, and locked it.

Then he stood back up and let out with an exceedingly loud "finally."

He then said good-bye to me in a very friendly way. For a long time I continued making my way along the Danube Canal—out of which the air was wafting the reflections of the palatial insurance headquarters and their lighted advertising signs reflected in the water—until the darkness of the current diffused my eyes.

# IN THE COURSE OF MY COURSES—FROM NEUWALDEGG TO SCHOTTENTOR

For years now I've been riding in *one of the red streetcars on the 43 line from the "Jörgerbad" station into town, to the department of musicology, and then from the Schottentor stop back out to Jörgerbad.*
One day I'm riding to the department of musicology as usual, just wanting to get where I have to go, but this particular car somehow seems to me as if it won't be able to make it; the straps are hanging with a very droopy look as they swing limply from their fastenings, while the pneumatic doors are flapping suspiciously, in the way shirts flap on a clothesline when it's windy, and it seems to me that all this rattling and clanking and flapping, far beyond normal bounds, is carrying over to the streetcar as a whole, the outer layer of skin over its frame suddenly striking me, when I take a quick sideways glance out of the window, as wrinkled-lined-shriveled, as if the whole car, hunching down into itself again and again, right there in the middle of the street, wanted to roll straight onto some pile of scrap metal heaped up like a dome.

That said, I have to consider that all the years I've spent so far at the University of Vienna have been a fantastic fraud, an unparalleled swindle, not needing—because of the extent of its deviousness and nastiness—to even think of taking a back seat to the economic and political kickback scandals involving corruption among Austrian construction firms, a fraud on my part against scholarship, which I believed I could attain to, as well as a fraud on the part of the scholarship held against me, which made me believe I was indispensable to it.

End of the line! the conductor yells; I push my way out of the streetcar and proceed onward and upward to the university, as on every other day; everything seems at the moment to have run its course again, but while I'm looking from a window in the corridor on the second floor how the sheen-glinting streetcar tracks, over and past the heat waves of which the multicolored swarms of butterflies aflutter in a summer bursting forth now are skimming and are woven into the air of this day like a many-colored pattern, alive and whirling, one of those dimwit assistants whom I still have to put up with suddenly draws me off to the side and whispers with a hoarse voice into my ear: I have a history of music for you; I'm holding a history of music for your use, so I think you should be grateful to me . . . Then he presses an envelope into my hand and vanishes into the nearest auditorium, awkwardly fleeing my glance as if he were embarrassed *by* me but at the same time even more *for* me.

When I open the envelope, I'm astonished to find *not* what I'd been expecting, which was one of the usual accounts of how someone is hoping to be able one day to complete *The Art of Fugue* with something approaching authenticity, *but rather an international medical claim form issued by the health-insurance department of Carinthia,* complete with a handwritten comment in pencil, "Not usable for us," and unmistakably issued in my name.

Although the next thing I had planned was to read to the empty seats in Auditorium I, as a stand-in for my professor, the concluding sections of his lectures on *The Development of the Toccata from Frescobaldi to J. S. Bach*, since my professor practically never shows up anymore, the idea being, as it was two years previously, to present this lecture material, which he had been giving over and over, exactly the same, word for word, every two years since the end of the Second World War, starting at the beginning and going on to the end, reading it out yet once more all over again, from start to finish, word for word, with no changes—or having it read out by one of his flunkey assistants, of whom I am one—during the course of which latter process he would insist on showing up in SS boots, taking out a metronome he'd brought with him, setting it to ♪ = 160, and waiting until it ran down, this procedure designed, as he would emphasize, to be able to ensure that this ritual progressed at the tempo of the "Waldstein" sonata; moreover, the professor required all the assistants representing him, like me, to bring a metronome to these presentations and, in the course of representing him, to set the metronome running at ♪ = 160, so as to be able to execute his text with authenticity before the empty seats in the lecture hall. So instead of going into Auditorium I that day, I immediately walk right out of the university.

As I leave the building through the main entrance, I don't, however, as expected and as I otherwise always would, make my way onto the Ring near Schottentor, but wind up instead, most unexpectedly, in some completely different place lying somewhere out past the university, quite far outlying, roughly up on the higher ground of Alser Strasse, as if I had just then been blown out of the injured wards and ruptured courts of the old General Hospital, blown far out and away, far out and up and away, almost all the way up to the Hernals Beltway!

Oftentimes I walk ceaselessly back and forth in my room for hours on end without knowing why, and while I'm ceaselessly walking back and forth in my room for hours on end again today, just now, without knowing why, I suddenly have to realize that my entire life up to this point has consisted of nothing other than a single, unmitigated act of endlessly walking back and forth for hours at a time in this enclosed space.

I look down at the dark spots with which the sidewalks and streets here are strewn, as if I were being drawn to the ground by these faint patterns of glinting mica eyes in the paving material.

At first I believe they are the remaining marks of large raindrops fallen out of the night onto the sidewalks and streets. But when the spots have not been absorbed by the heat of midday, I can only think that the sidewalks and streets are constantly being spit on in profusion by the burning sky of the given day or, much more likely, by the good people of Vienna themselves, the latter speculation making it no surprise at all to me that these blotches never disappear.

Lately I often have the suspicion and the feeling that from the Vienna roofs of the sky above the city I'm often—far too often—being deliberately spit on, really and truly *spit down on*.

For that matter, too, when the city government for unknown reasons keeps so many rows of street lights burning bright by day.

## ATTEMPT TO BREAK OUT TO KLOSTERNEUBURG

Many days begin in the morning as if they were already at an end. The beams of fog form footpaths on which there's no negotiating, and the "light"—if it can be called that—of a night by now depleted and washed out smudges itself like mold onto the walls of buildings, which then, touched by the gray of morning, soon start crumbling all the faster, passing thereby into a yet more frenzied process of decay than would be the case otherwise.

It was on a such a day that I boarded a streetcar of the D line at Schottentor and rode to Nussdorf, where I then waited for one of the busses of the Dr. Richard transportation company that went to Klosterneuburg.

While waiting for the Dr. Richard bus to Klosterneuburg I suddenly felt the need to undertake a closer observation of the Nussdorf station, especially the pissoir with its tar paper walls that spread an ammonia-like odor through the toilet area.

The public Viennese pissoirs in the old art-nouveau stations along the city rail system are a thing of utmost mysteriousness. Something like yellow lime clings to the tar paper walls, torn prophylactics are often found in the grates over the drains, the drains are often stopped up so that the whole pissoir is flooded with diluted urine, and attached to the walls are brass plates on which it is brought to the attention of visitors that, for reasons of propriety, all garments are to be fastened and put into order before leaving the convenience, while all around innumerable people have scratched their names and their depictions of human sex organs—transfigured through the simple grace of unsophisticated folk art—into the slimy, shiny coating of tar, oftentimes, too, at so great a height that a ladder at least two or three meters tall would be required to adorn practically the topmost reaches of the space, all the way to the ceiling, with drawings and writings.

I was afraid someone might suddenly come in, threaten me, knock me down, land a blow on the back of my head or give my neck a nasty chop with the edge of his hand so that my face or even my whole head would wind up awash in the urine draining away.

I have often feared that someone—someone who had been skulking behind me for a long time, just waiting for me—would suddenly enter the toilet and finally approach me. They say men have often been observed spending whole days and weeks in public conveniences, mostly hiding somewhere in a corner so as not to draw that much attention to themselves but sometimes also standing right at the drainage trough so as to observe their urinating neighbors left and right as closely as possible. I was often afraid of being beaten up by somebody like that, and my face or even my whole head would then be washed away in the flowing urine.

This disease of the art-nouveau pissiors in Vienna—so easy to pick up!

I brought my visit to the public convenience in the Nussdorf station to an end without having encountered any habitual denizen of the premises, left the station by going through the empty waiting room, in which cigarette butts from the night before were still lying on the greasy floor, and then the Dr. Richard bus came, I got on, bought a ticket, and rode to Klosterneuburg.

I do not go, as I had originally intended, to see the monastery or the church; I take the railroad underpass to the Danube instead.

I'll mention the small garden plots, the wooden huts in those gardens, a setting divided into lines of unreadable writing, signs saying Protected Area—Ground Water! Entry and Contamination in any Form Prohibited!, the fenced-in wells and springs, the meltwater from the mountainous foothills around Vienna hollowing out the road from below, and lying around here and there discarded, rusted gasoline containers, broken jelly jars among the bushes, also feather dusters, pieces of tile, telephone booths with no telephone, all sinking into the swamp here, and finally a notice about collapsed sandpits.

At the bank of the Danube I find the chain ferry "not in operation"; in the beams of the little house in which up till not long ago you would buy your tickets for the crossing, except you can't buy tickets now because the ferry is no longer in operation, a swarm of wasps had nested and then frozen rigid and breakable as glass during the past winter, and sometimes I see through their transparent covering one of the insects frostily crumpled, now dangling from the beams in the cold of the winter gone by. The coffee shop at the Old Chain Ferry has burnt down, half the building charred, a smell of ashes on the terrace. What I would very much like is to describe to you in more detail the silos and the tanks at the Korneuburg refinery on the opposite bank of the Danube and to mention as part of the picture a passing barge, then to have this description depict a boat "drawing a black line through the hammered metal of the river" as well, but I'm drawn back in the direction of Klosterneuburg, walking along a street being hollowed out by the meltwater from the mountainous foothills around Vienna, and then I encounter a workman digging away at a pile of sand—in all likelihood unloaded here at the side of the road from a dump truck while I was spending time on the bank of the Danube—by taking his shovel and shoveling the sand from the road into the swampy ground and into the meltwater from the mountainous foothills around Vienna that's hollowing out the streets and roads but is here just flowing through the swamp.

The sand trickles from the road into the ditch, covers the flowing meltwater for a short time, and it looks as if the sand could absorb that flowing meltwater; the sand, I tell myself, will contain and cover the meltwater, and that's really how it looks, I think; everything is pointing that way, but then the water starts flowing again, and it's not the sand that's absorbing the water but the water the sand.

The ceaseless repetition of this process is causing the workman to shovel harder and harder, faster and faster, which then makes the sand trickle faster and faster, in more and more of a blur, and while observing all this I also can't help seeing that the water is beginning to flow correspondingly faster and faster and is thus continuing to hollow out the streets and roads.

I speak to the workman in words more or less to this effect:

"Excuse me. Striking up a conversation with a person I don't know is just not something I do; in fact, I consider it outrageously rude to start talking to a person who doesn't know me and whom I don't know," I tell him, and I could count on the fingers of one hand the times I've spoken to people I don't know, for only when it is absolutely necessary would I ever address a stranger.

"Now, however," I go on to explain, "while watching you do your work, which appears entirely futile to me, at least right now, I feel a need to point out to you that the whole nature of your activity fills me with sorrow."

The workman continues shoveling the sand from the sandpile by the roadside into the ditch, and when there's no more sand, no more sandpile lying by the roadside, then they'll transport a second sandpile to him, or they'll have him shovel sand from some other sandpile into who knows what somewhere else.

He stops working, gives me a friendly look, and says it doesn't bother him at all, not one bit, that I simply start talking to him; he had been wanting to take a short "breather" anyway, and now he has a reason or a welcome excuse not only to plan a "breather" but actually to take one.

The workman leans on the handle of his shovel and "breathes."

Meanwhile, like a flash of lightning, almost frightened, the water has stopped its flowing and the sand its trickling.

What did I want to know? he asks.

When would the chain ferry be operating again? I ask.

First, he answers, he doesn't know anything about a chain ferry; he's never even heard there was a chain ferry around here, and second, if this chain ferry exists, he has no way of knowing when it's running and when it's not, because first he's never heard of such a ferry, let alone ever seen it, and second he's working in this area for the first time today and all they did was dump the sandpile in front on him and leave it to him to work on.

He gives me a piece of good advice—to ask in the tourist office at

Klosterneuburg, for they're the people who should know; it's their responsibility to.

I thank him for the suggestion, apologize again for having just struck up a conversation like that, and say good-bye, whereupon he resumes his work of shoveling sand from the sandpile at the side of the road into the swampy ground of the ditch, and as if on command the water once more starts flowing and the sand once more trickling . . .

For the whole rest of the day I won't be able to put the thought of that sand shoveling out of my mind, I'm thinking as the part of Klosterneuburg where the garden plots are laid out comes closer to me and I'm reminded, to my astonishment, by this particular setting, divided as it is into lines of unreadable writing, lines filled in with wooden huts and small garden houses, some falling apart, some carefully maintained, of certain mathematical phenomena inexplicable to me, of mysterious conundrums in the nature of endless geometric equations and calculations of coordinates.

I return to my starting point, but I never get to describe in any greater detail either the yellow telephoneless telephone booths now sinking into the ground or the garden-plot setting divided into lines of unreadable writing, because I'm suddenly seized by the suspicion, one I keep harboring, that the people in this area are "air talkers." Several things point in that direction, it seems to me; I can hear glittering nagging sounds wandering at large and rising up to the sky, floating in the air, and I'm afraid one of them could try accosting me.

But not a one is in evidence; instead, a dog comes bolting out from an open garden gate, barks at me, jumps up almost to my throat, and my whole body starts to shake. Of course the dog can tell at once that I'm afraid of it, whereupon it harasses me even more, because the more you're afraid of a dog, the more forcefully it will come after you.

This darting, yapping large terrier starts biting at my pants, and all I can think is that I'm a ridiculous individual as far as this dog is concerned; he's tugging at my pants, and any minute now he'll tear them, rip them to pieces.

Finally I hear a piercing whistle from inside the house in the garden. The dog immediately stops biting at my pants, runs back into the garden, disappears into his doghouse, and lets out a contented howl.

I go to continue on my way, but before I can start moving a man with a paunchy stomach, whose round glasses don't seem to fit his red, puffy face at all, appears from inside the small garden house, comes up to me, apologizes politely for the episode with the dog, which he's really displeased with himself about, for it can only be attributed to his negligence in having forgotten to close the garden gate so that his dog was able to run out and harass me, but he's just arrived from the city, where he owns a wine storehouse and a shop in which he also sells the wine, so he's a wine merchant and has just now come from the wine shop and storehouse in the city back to his garden-plot house and has, as only too often, he was sorry to say, forgotten to close the garden gate behind him, which his dog probably noticed at once and—again at once—used his opportunity, his inconveniently convenient opportunity, to full advantage by seizing on it to harass me.

"A very lively animal, you know, with an overdeveloped sense of play, very nervous but otherwise harmless, except for one thing, you know, just one thing: he always goes after pants; he's absolutely crazy about biting people's pants; I'd even call him a passionate pants biter. Sometimes I toss him a pair of my old pants that I can't wear for work anymore, just so he can have a chance once in a while to shred a pair of pants to rags. I'm surprised, incidentally, that my dog didn't tear your pants to shreds while he was at it, because in most cases he'll tear a pair of pants apart within seconds without my being able to stop him, so I believe you could say you've had good luck, since your pants are still in one piece. What I'm noticing just now is that you wear very wide pants, which makes it all the more surprising that my dog spared them, because he's a passionate devotee of wide pants, the wider the better, ones preferably flapping in the wind, and the wider the given pair of pants, the quicker they're chewed up by my dog, and from the radius of the pants legs, as well as from the strength of the wind in which they're flapping, you can read the capacity and intensity of the speed with which he starts nipping and yipping. And that's why I wear pants as wide as yours so that when I can't wear them to work in anymore I can toss the widest available pants to my dog, just so that he can have a chance to shred to rags as many pairs of pants as possible as often as possible. So it's good that at the last minute I was able to keep him from shredding your pants, because otherwise you would suddenly have been standing there with no pants on," the wine merchant says.

I accept the wine merchant's invitation to have a glass of the "pride of his cellar," but I regret it the very next moment.

"You know," he says, "I'm not very well liked around here; in fact I'm extremely disliked. Why that is I can't explain to myself, especially because a wine merchant usually enjoys the highest of respect in his village or town, since the residents of the place normally have to depend on their local wine merchant or their wine shops. Even though I constantly keep good reserves of wine stored in Vienna—the best wines in Europe, for that matter—I enjoy no respect at all here, but I mean absolutely none whatever. Around here it seems to be standard practise to plot against wine merchants, and it's practically an absolute rule that I'm ruthlessly passed over and ignored. Perhaps I'm held in contempt because I'm not from around here; I'm a Viennese, and everyone else, whether we're talking about owners of garden plots or what they call "do-it-yourself house builders," is from Klosterneuburg, not Vienna, so for these people I'm probably an annoying foreign presence.

"What's more, the 'do-it-yourselfers'—at least that's what they call them—stole quite a large supply of lumber from me one night, just plain carted it away behind my back! One morning I leave my house and go to check out the quality of the lumber I had bought earlier, go to the place where I had had them stack it, and what do I see—you'll be surprised: not a scrap of lumber, nothing that would indicate any wood had ever been there; even the sawdust and shavings were gone; instead of seeing a place filled with lumber, I see a completely woodless spot on the ground. I'm exposed to this persecution with no means of defense, and these people are trying everything in their power to drive me out of the area; they stop at nothing. But I won't let myself be driven out of the area; not for a king's ransom will I let myself be driven out, and even though this part of the world disgusts me more and more, I'm going to stay here purely for spite and lead what to all appearances is a pleasant life, just to show the people here that you can't simply drive someone out, and I'll show these people that I won't let my life be ruined, because it's important, always and everywhere, and from the very start, to show people that you just will not put up with anything whatsoever."

During the wine merchant's harangue I remember that I'd had a dream about my scalp the night before.

In the dream I could see my own scalp with large white circles on it. I shook the white circles out of my hair so that it began snowing from my scalp, for winter had set in with full force on the plateau of my skull.

While the wine merchant goes on talking, the memory of the dream dominates me until I can no longer listen to a word he's saying, because I see before me once more the January of my hair, and then the large white circles vanish, just disappear; white dots and specks are all that's left. I try removing those white dots and specks from my scalp by scratching them all away, but while I set out—believing that I've at last removed the first white dot or speck—to scratch the next one loose, I discover that the first one, which I previously thought I'd removed, is again clearly in evidence, right where it was before. So then I restrict myself to whisking away only the first speck or dot from now on, concentrating on just this one small dot of life because I know it would again be clearly in evidence if I were to set out to remove the next speck, whereas it's important at this moment that at least *one* white speck or dot should be absent from my scalp. Then I notice the absurdity of trying to remove even one single speck or dot from the high plateau of my skull, since all those white dots or specks are growing increasingly large, until each one is at least half the size of my whole scalp, and I marvel that it's even possible to find room for so many halfscalpsized dots and specks on my scalp. Then I notice that in reality my scalp is nothing but one single large white speck, a frozen roof of snow, winter over my thoughts.

After his portrayals of the intrigues and persecutions to which he is exposed with no means of defense, the wine merchant asks me in a sly sort of way what I'm doing in this area in the first place, what business I have here, what the reason for my presence is, and I answer him that I came because of the chain ferry, I'm concerned purely with the chain ferry, but now I have to leave right away, this minute; an important appointment following my visit here is the reason I have to go away at once,

and I do go away at once, not without having said good-bye; but no, I don't go, I run, ride back at once on one of those days that have ended before they even began,

on this eveninglikemorningishly afternoonnight;

in fact, this day hasn't even dawned yet.

## PHILOSOPHY OF HOUSEHOLD MANAGEMENT, HERNALS-STYLE

Brown window frames are a landmark of Hernals.

All the window frames in Hernals are painted brown, and I can't remember ever having seen any window frames that weren't painted brown.

Not only by the brown window frames themselves but also by the odor that makes its way out of the windows framed by the brown-painted window frames can I recognize every time without fail that I'm in Hernals and nowhere else, because I know I can't be anywhere else, because I know it's impossible for me to be anywhere else.

Even when the odor is of pancakes, potato salad, or fried meat patties, I know—that is, my nose can sense without fail—that it's a Hernals odor, has to be a Hernals odor, because it's not even remotely possible for it not to be a Hernals odor.

Anywhere other than in Hernals, potato salad smells like potato salad, whereas potato salad in Hernals smells like Hernals. Hernals potato salad.

Hernals potato salad smells like Hernals exactly the same as a Hernals Wiener schnitzel smells like Hernals.

That Hernals odor probably has to do with the masonry walls in Hernals, the back courtyards in Hernals, the streets in Hernals, the sewers in Hernals, and the taverns in Hernals, at least enough so that a person realizes at once it's a Hernals odor, just as it's entirely possible to tell the difference between a Hernals sewer or a Hernals tavern and a sewer not located in Hernals or a tavern not located in Hernals.

In the entrance courts and back courtyards of Hernals people string clotheslines, and I know at once that these clotheslines they string in the courtyards of Hernals are typical Hernals clotheslines and that the clothes hung out to dry here in the courtyards of Hernals but then dirtied all over again by the soot in the air of Hernals are Hernals clothes, unmistakably Hernals clothes!

The combination parking garage and gas station opposite the building I live in is indisputably a Hernals combination parking garage and gas station, and it's impossible to believe that the attendant's laughter, the attendant's dirty jokes, the attendant's rosy pink cheeks, the fleshy bags under his eyes or the puffiness around his lips or his red, swollen nose can be any kind other than Hernals laughter, any kind other than Hernals dirty jokes, any kind other than Hernals rosy pink cheeks, not possibly any kind other than typical Hernals fleshy bags under the attendant's eyes and puffiness around his lips, and it would be absolutely inconceivable to think that the attendant's red, swollen nose could under any circumstances whatever be any kind other than a Hernals red, swollen nose, for such red, swollen noses can protrude from the face like that only in Hernals, and I can't remember ever having seen anywhere else noses swollen in quite this same way.

Now and then I hear dishes clattering, women scolding, and water running whenever someone turns on a tap.

From time to time I connect the brown window frames and dirty house walls not just with Hernals, but also with Ottakring and Favoriten.

And sometimes I also connect the landmarks of Hernals with all of Vienna, Lower Austria, and Styria.

And what also happens oftentimes is that I feel as if all of Austria and Europe were just Hernals, one single Hernals.

Then I get the feeling that the world shouldn't be called the world but would have to be called Hernals instead, a "Hernals globe" orbiting the sun.

I had set some flower pots onto the window sill across from my apartment door in the hallway. I watered the sprouting plants and the flowers in the pots every day. But the neighbors damaged the sprouts, broke off the flowers, pulled the roots out of the soil, and threw the pots, along with the soil, out of the hallway window into the courtyard. The next day the building superintendent bawled me out and charged me with unbelievably shameless behavior and absolutely outrageous conduct—throwing anything at all out of the hallway window into the courtyard was prohibited in the first place, of course; that why they had trash cans, and *what* did I think the trash cans were *for*, and on top of that I had taken it upon myself to throw perfectly good flower pots out of the hallway window into the courtyard, with all the noise and dirt that went with it, and now, even though he had swept the whole courtyard just yesterday, he was going to have to sweep it all over again today, but he wasn't going to anyway and in fact wouldn't think for even one single split second of doing so, but I should do it instead or else he would notify the owner, and the owner would then most certainly cancel my lease, which would suit him just fine, because then he and the other tenants would then be rid of me, slob that I am, once and for all, and if he should really wind up being forced to sweep the courtyard once again in case I wasn't willing to sweep the courtyard myself, why then I'd have to pay him to sweep the courtyard all over again, etc., etc.

Since that time I don't put flowers out onto the hallway window any more; I've given up putting flowers onto the hallway window, because it makes no sense to put flowers onto the hallway window, no, it's not just senseless, but impossible, for that matter, since it's not a common thing to set flowers onto hallway windows, and setting flowers onto hallway windows can even be grounds for having your lease cancelled.

Every time I enter my building, make my way through the stairwells, and open my apartment door, all the other apartment doors open too, and the people come out or look suspiciously through the cracks in their doors as if it were somehow rude or arrogant of me to set foot inside the building at all, let alone to take it upon myself to open my apartment door.

Often someone will knock on my door or ring the bell. I open up to greet my visitor, but there's no visitor waiting at the door; there's nobody there. One or another of the neighbors is always knocking at my door or ringing my bell, just to disturb me. Often in the middle of the night.

Lately, whenever somebody knocks or rings, I don't even open the door; in fact I don't go to the door at all anymore; I refuse to go to the door or to open the door, because I know there won't be any visitor waiting at the door; instead, all that's happened is that one of the neighbors has maliciously rung or knocked just to make a fool out of me, trying to get me to open up by this malicious ringing.

My footsteps crossing the vestibule are monitored and tracked with utmost precision, and when I leave the building, all the windows open so everyone can watch me as I go away.

They're afraid I'm going to take the mats away from their doors; they have a persistent fear that somebody might steal their doormats.

Many of them go so far as to take their doormats into their apartments after they've wiped their feet so as to be completely sure no one can steal their doormats.

Such are the customs in Hernals, the traditions in Hernals, the ingrained habits in Hernals, the folkways in Hernals, the common usage in Hernals, the folkways *and* the common usage in Hernals.

In any building you enter the doors will open when you go through the hallway or the stairwell; doors open everywhere, people look out or come out, step resolutely right into your path, look at you suspiciously and ask what you're doing here. The lives of these people in Hernals are just this kind of constant "opendoor-closedoorslyness"!

Often, people will toss opened, spoiled, stinking cans of food and other garbage in front of my door. The cans of spoiled food rust and burst open in front of my door and dirty the hallway.

Then the superintendent starts chastising me for tossing everything outside in front of my door onto his nice clean hallway, all freshly washed and scrubbed. And if I should protest against his indictment, he just goes on chastising: it's a filthy rotten disgrace that I should accuse the other people living in the building of such abominations!

But how do I know this wasn't done by people from one or other of the buildings nearby?

Why people from Vienna, for that matter?

Why shouldn't it be that somebody in Linz might have gone to his trash can early in the morning, taken it to the main train station in Linz, traveled—along with said trash can—to the West Station in Vienna, gotten out, ridden the city rail line to the *Alser Strasse* station, continued from there to the square called *Elterlein Platz*, then proceeded on foot to Blumen Gasse and walked up to the second floor of this building so as finally to end up trundling this garbage off to the one place where it really seems most to belong: in front of *your* apartment door!

# JÖRGER STRASSE PRELUDE AND HERNALS BELTWAY FUGUE

Dear Sir:

Can you still remember last Sunday? Didn't you suddenly start to feel in the mood to go to a bakery? An outright craving or not? So then you did go—or so I'm assured over and over from reliable sources—into a bakery on Jörger Strasse, didn't you? You'd probably never been there in your life before, because my father, who's a regular customer in that shop, practically a fixture, saw you there that day for the first time.

So then you did open the glass door of the bakery while casting a sideways look, on an angle, over toward the *green and red imitation artificial natural objects made of sweeteners and confectionery* in the display window. And were you not then actually inside the bakery and suddenly seated on a padded red plastic chair, and did you in all likelihood not even really take notice of your closingtheglassdoorbehindyou, your enteringthecoffeehouse-aroma, lookingforandchoosingaseat, goingovertooneofthosepaddedredplasticchairs and the seating of your person in such a way that it seemed to you as if nothing like this had ever occurred before because all this while you were continuing to look at the *imitation artificial natural objects made of sweeteners and confectionery* in the bakery window and afterwards retaining a color negative image of them on your retina? Is this the only way you can explain to yourself how it was that you were all of a sudden seated on a padded red plastic chair without having walked up to the chair beforehand and taken a seat? You did then order a jelly doughnut, after all, ate it, and drank a glass of water with it, but you were very soon outside the bakery again, probably because you couldn't put up with that sickeningly sweet coffee odor any more, which I can understand. Yes, you paid your check and left the shop at once.

Right ahead of you, though, an older gentleman with a black hat and a black coat left the shop, in his hands a package of sweets wrapped in paper with the name of that bakery on Jörger Strasse on it—do you remember?—the gentleman was holding the package flat or horizontally in his hands, using his hands as a surface to support his package, both hands, which is why he was unable to open the door of the shop by himself, because he needed both hands to carry the package of sweets and hence had neither hand free to manage the handle of the bakery door, which was why a salesgirl dressed in pink and wearing a small circular apron around her midsection (radius of the apron about 25 centimeters) came to his aid, at least to the extent of opening the door for him so he could leave the bakery. You left the shop right behind him without the door closing first, because you relieved the salesgirl dressed in pink of the handle of the still open door, went out onto Jörger Strasse, probably with a sour aftertaste in your mouth from whatever remaining bits of the jelly doughnut might have been stuck in your teeth. You were walking along behind the gentleman (headed for the Hernals Beltway) and saw him turn his glance left to look into the display window. The old gentleman walking ahead of you was examining the *red and green artificial imitation natural objects made of sweeteners and confectionery* in the window. Then he turned his eyes straight ahead again, since he had now put behind him the length of seven or so meters along which the show window faces the sidewalk, after which the sidewalk no longer presented the display to his view but only a stretch of gray, dirty building fronts instead. Indeed, he most likely turned his head to face directly forward once more because he was in no mood to subject his eyes to the sight of gray, dirty building fronts. It was just beyond that length of display window that you wanted to pass the old man, because he was walking rather slowly. But just at the moment you were speeding up your pace as part of your passing maneuver you saw the old gentleman lean against the dirty gray wall of the building, and then he fell down (!)—do you remember?—and upon impact on the concrete sidewalk the back of his head probably caused a thud like a muffled drumbeat! If you hadn't stepped aside briskly, he would have fallen directly up against you, would have taken you down to the ground with him, you would have been lying there on the ground exactly the same way, and the back of your head hitting the concrete sidewalk would presumably also have caused a thud like a drumbeat similar to the one caused by back of the gentleman's head hitting the concrete sidewalk. Like a wooden board that's been hastily leaned against a wall and thus falls over with a loud thump—that's how the old gentleman hastily leaned against the dirty gray building wall and then fell over backwards with a loud thump. Quite a large crowd of people gathered at once, and someone tried to pilfer the package of sweets wrapped in paper with the name of that bakery on Jörger Strasse on it that the old gentleman was still holding in his hands, in both hands, but that wasn't possible, because the hands of the gentleman lying on the ground would not release the package, his whole body now being perfectly stiff, as if he had suddenly turned to wood, transformed himself into a veritable assemblage of wooden boards.

To someone from among the people who had all of a sudden gathered around the old gentleman lying stiffly on the ground, in his hands the package of sweets wrapped in paper with the name of that bakery on Jörger Strasse on it, which he was clutching so tightly in his hands that it would have been impossible to wrest it away from him, to someone in the crowd that had gathered to observe the gentleman lying on the ground it occurred that somebody should do something; something really ought to be done, said a man in the crowd that had gathered to have a look at the gentleman lying on the ground, a man to whom the thought had come that something should be done. The man to whom the thought had come that something needed to be done ran to a telephone booth on the nearby Hernals Beltway and probably notified the rescue squad while the rest of the people who had gathered around just kept standing there watching the old gentleman lying on the ground.

However, when the man from the crowd to whom it had occurred that something should be done had run off to a telephone booth on the nearby Hernals Beltway, presumably to notify the rescue squad, when the man from the crowd that had gathered and subsequently grown two or three times larger, all to have a look at the old gentleman lying on the ground and holding in his hands a package of sweets wrapped in paper with the name of that bakery on Jörger Strasse on it so tightly that it would have been impossible to wrest it away from him, when the man from the crowd that had gathered and subsequently grown four times larger, all to observe the gentleman lying there on the ground on his back, in his hands a package of sweets wrapped in paper with the name of that bakery on Jörger Strasse on it, the package clutched so tightly that it would have been impossible to wrest it away from him, when the man had just run off, the old gentleman lying on the ground on his back s u d d e n l y  g o t  u p, just suddenly stood back up, just simply stood back up without so much as a by-your-leave, stood up and observed the crowd of people which had gathered to observe him who had only shortly before been lying on the ground on his back, in his hands a package of sweets wrapped in paper with the name of that bakery on Jörger Strasse on it, observed the observers with interest and asked what was going on, what had happened that a crowd of people had suddenly gathered and was looking at something, whatever it was, with such interest, because it seemed very peculiar to him, the gentleman said, since he had simply left the bakery on Jörger Strasse, walked along Jörger Strasse heading for the nearby Hernals Beltway, and all of a sudden there was a crowd of people gathered and looking at something with interest, a crowd of people all looking without so much as a by-your-leave at some particular point, and he for one found it peculiar and passing strange, the gentleman declared, that he had not even noticed this activity of a whole crowd of people all gathered without so much as a by-your-leave and looking with interest and intense concentration at some particular point.

The crowd of people that had gathered without so much as a by-your-leave answered with frosty silence the questions of the old gentleman, who had stood back up without so much as a by-your-leave, and the crowd that had gathered without so much as a by-your-leave and looked on with interest and intense concentration now began slowly breaking up, and at the end you and the old gentleman were standing alone facing one another and looking at one another like two bulls eyeing one another as if each were seeing in the other a new barn door, one bull looking at the other bull as if each were seeing in the other a new barn door, each standing and facing the other like two bulls in front of two new barn doors, as if they were two bulls each eyeing the other like a new barn door—that was how you kept eyeing the old gentleman, that is to say as if he were a new barn door, and that was how the old gentleman kept eyeing you, dear sir, as if you were a new barn door, you standing and facing him like a bull in front of a new barn door and he in turn standing and facing you like a bull in front of a new barn door, right there on Jörger Strasse, almost at the nearby Hernals Beltway.

And while you were standing there facing one another, the old gentleman suddenly began talking; oh yes, he did. He asked you this question: "Can you—inasmuch as you are the only person remaining out of the crowd of people at first having gathered without so much as a by-your-leave and looked on with interest and intense concentration, only then to break up again, likewise without so much as a by-your-leave—perhaps give me some explanation of the incident that just took place here and that for that matter might still be taking place, because, you see, all I did was simply leave the bakery on Jörger Strasse, holding in my hands a package of sweets wrapped in paper with the name of the store on it, walk along Jörger Strasse toward the nearby Hernals Beltway, and all of a sudden a crowd of people gathered and observed something with

interest; I find it odd that I was u n a b l e  e i t h e r  t o  o b s e r v e
o r  i n  a n y  o t h e r  w a y  t o  n o t i c e  how this crowd looking with intense concentration gathered to begin with, because the
people went away and vanished just as suddenly as they had appeared and stood there, and you are the only person left, so perhaps
you know more about the incident that attracted all those people."
You answered the old gentleman by saying that you couldn't tell
him any more than what had taken place as you saw it with your
own eyes, and so you could only attempt to describe the whole set
of circumstances, in that way making every effort to fill in with
as few gaps as possible the incidents that had occurred or that for
that matter might still be occurring. Did you not say more or less
word for word the following to the old gentleman?—"Went to the
bakery today, felt in the mood to go to the bakery, an outright craving, let me tell you! Was in the bakery on Jörger Strasse for the first
time today after never having been there before in my whole life.
Opened the glass door while at the same time casting a sideways
look, on an angle, over toward the green and red imitation artificial
natural objects made of sweeteners and confectionery in the display
window. Was then suddenly inside the bakery and seated on a padded red plastic chair without having gone in or taken a seat. Didn't
even really take notice of my closingtheglassdoorbehindme, my
enteringthecoffeehouse-aroma, my lookingforandchoosingaseat,
my goingovertooneofthosepaddedredplasticchairs and my seating myself, because during that whole time I was l o o k i n g
o v e r  a t  t h e  r e d  a n d  g r e e n  i m i t a t i o n  a r t i f i c i a l
n a t u r a l  o b j e c t s  m a d e  o f  s w e e t e n e r s  a n d  t h e n
a f t e r w a r d s  r e t a i n i n g  t h e m  o n  m y  r e t i n a  a l l  t h e
w h i l e  a s  a  c o l o r  n e g a t i v e  i m a g e . This is the only way

I can explain to myself how I was suddenly sitting there without having taken a seat. Then ordered a jelly doughnut in that bakery, ate it, and drank a glass of water with it, but then left the shop soon after that, because I couldn't put up with that sickeningly sweet coffee odor anymore. Paid and got out. Then saw you, to whom I'm describing all this, for the first time. You left the bakery just ahead of me, after all, in your hands a package of sweets wrapped in paper with the name of that bakery on it; you were holding the package flat or horizontally in both hands, using your hands as a surface to support your package, and I could see exactly how it was that you were unable to open the door of the bakery by yourself, since you needed both hands to carry the package and hence had neither hand free to manage the brass-colored door handle, which was why a pink salesgirl wearing a small half-circle apron (radius of the apron about 25 centimeters) opened the door for you, thereby enabling you to leave the bakery. I then left the shop right behind you, in my mouth a sour aftertaste from whatever remaining bits of the jelly doughnut had stuck in my teeth. Then I was walking along behind you (headed for the Hernals Beltway) and saw you examining the r e d   a n d   g r e e n   a r t i f i c i a l   i m i t a t i o n   n a t u r a l o b j e c t s   m a d e   o f   s w e e t e n e r s  in the display window. Wanted to pass you just then, because I thought you were walking too slowly, you understand, but just at the moment I sped up my pace as part of my passing maneuver you leaned against the dirty gray wall of the building and then suddenly toppled over backwards, just fell right down, the impact of the back of your head on the concrete sidewalk giving out a muffled thud like a drumbeat. If I hadn't stepped aside briskly, you would have fallen right up against me, you're thinking. At once there gathered quite a large crowd of people, and someone tried to pilfer from you the package of sweets wrapped in paper with the name of that bakery on Jörger Strasse on it that you were still holding in your hands, but that wasn't possible, in all probability because it was felt to be most awkward for you, situated as you were, to have held and for that matter still to be holding a package in your hands, but it proved impossible to take the package out of your hands, because you were holding onto it as tightly, your whole body now perfectly stiff, as if it had turned to wood, to a wooden frame or stand. To someone from among the people who had gathered to see you lying stiffly on the ground, to observe and have a look, it suddenly occurred that something should be done; that something really ought to be done is a thought that occurred to someone, and the someone to whom the thought came that something should be done, yes this very man who had had that thought then took that thought and ran with it to the nearby Hernals Beltway, presumably to notify the rescue squad. At the very moment, however, when the man had run off to the nearby Hernals Beltway, you suddenly got back up, just stood up again all of a sudden, looked with great interest at the people looking on with such great interest, asked them what had happened, what had taken place, for you found it odd that all you did was simply go out of the bakery on Jörger Strasse, walk along Jörger Strasse heading for the nearby Hernals Beltway, and suddenly there was a crowd of people gathered and looking at something with great interest and intense concentration, which you thought peculiar, you said, because you had been completely unable to take note of this activity of people gathering. The crowd of people looking on with interest answered your questions with frosty silence and began breaking up; by the end, we were standing facing one another, alone, staring at one another like two bulls looking at two new barn doors. You then asked me what had happened, if I could give you some explanation, whereupon I told you everything I've just said, and with that I must come to an end, because I have attempted to describe the facts to you only from a personal standpoint and only to the extent of my capability."

Did the old gentleman not thereupon thank you very courteously, and did he not then reply more or less word for word with the following?—

"I believe your statement has given me enough to solve the mystery. Two parts of what you had to say clarify the whole thing for me: first you said at the beginning that you went into the bakery, casting while you were opening the glass door a sideways look, on an angle, at the r e d   a n d   g r e e n   i m i t a t i o n   a r t i f i c i a l   n a t u r a l   o b j e c t s   m a d e   o f   s w e e t e n e r s; as you said, you were then suddenly seated inside, on a padded red plastic chair without having taken a seat, because you were all the while continuing to look at the r e d   a n d   g r e e n   i m i t a t i o n   a r t i f i c i a l   n a t u r a l   o b j e c t s   m a d e   o f   s w e e t e n e r s and afterwards retained them on your retina as a color negative image; only in this way, you explained to me, would you be able to explain to yourself how it was that you were simply seated there without being able to remember having taken a seat. Then, as you explained to me, you left the shop behind me, headed toward the Hernals Beltway, and you observed me as I was taking a look at the r e d   a n d   g r e e n   a r t i f i c i a l   i m i t a t i o n   n a t u r a l   o b j e c t s   m a d e   o f   s w e e t e n e r s.

"So the solution of the mystery is as follows: just as you did not even notice that you had taken a seat, even though you know perfectly well that you must have taken a seat, since you were sitting there, albeit you were all the while continuing to glance over at the r e d   a n d   g r e e n   i m i t a t i o n   a r t i f i c i a l   n a t u r a l o b j e c t s   m a d e   o f   s w e e t e n e r s in the display window and then retained them on your retina as a color negative image, exactly so did I neither notice that I fell over backwards, nor that a crowd of people looking on with interest gathered for that reason, nor that I got up again, because I was all the while continuing to observe the   r e d   a n d   g r e e n   i m i t a t i o n   a r t i f i c i a l n a t u r a l   o b j e c t s   m a d e   o f   s w e e t e n e r s   and afterwards retaining them on my retina as a color negative image. The measure in which you were transfigured with befuddlement by the red and green artificial imitation natural objects made of sweeteners in the display window of the bakery is the measure of my having likewise been transfigured with befuddlement by these imitation natural objects made of sweeteners, so that I did not notice that a crowd of people had gathered around me and then broken up. Don't you think all of this tops everything for stupidity?!"

Of course you thought it all topped everything for stupidity, you replied to the old gentleman, and you both kept standing there facing one another the whole time, when suddenly a green rescue-squad ambulance with a blue revolving light came driving up and stopped next to you both. A very agitated driver got out and asked what happened and where the old man was lying; someone had called from a telephone booth on the Hernals Beltway and described how an old man had collapsed in the middle of the sidewalk and was lying right there in the middle of the sidewalk on Jörger Strasse, by the bakery. The old man explained as follows to the ambulance driver: "You have fallen victim to a regrettable mistake; I'm very sorry, but"—the old gentleman then pointed his index finger at you—"this gentleman is my witness; I was in the bakery, then I left the bakery; this gentleman happened to be walking behind me; I was admiring the red and green artificial imitation natural objects made of sweeteners in the display window of the bakery, and after that I don't know anything. This gentleman was so obliging as to describe to me what took place. I supposedly fell down suddenly and lay there perfectly stiff; then, to the astonishment of the people who had gathered around me, I suddenly got back up. If this gentleman had not told me the whole story, I would know nothing whatever about it. Don't you think it all tops everything for stupidity?"

Yes, of course it tops everything for stupidity, the ambulance driver agreed, but wouldn't you like to come along with me for at least a quick examination, the ambulance driver said to the old gentleman, because it could very well be the case that he had undergone a slight concussion through the impact of his head on the hard concrete of the sidewalk; but the old gentleman replied no, he did not believe he had suffered a concussion, because he felt right as rain, tiptop, in fact; just the way a fish feels in water is the way he was feeling here and now on Jörger Strasse, so it would be quite out of the question, the gentleman declared to the ambulance driver, that he should simply go with him for no reason, because he had a little grandson waiting for him at home and he wanted to bring him something, had made a special trip to the bakery for that reason and the package of sweets he was carrying in his hands was for his grandson, so now he had to bring the package wrapped in paper with the name of that bakery on

Jörger Strasse on it home to his grandson, since the grandson was waiting for it but having a hard time doing so, which meant no, there was no way he would go with the ambulance driver, mainly because of his grandson, but he furthermore did not believe he had a concussion; on the contrary, in fact, for he was feeling perfectly clear. Well, yes, the ambulance driver answered, that's what so many people have said—about feeling right as rain and all tiptop—but then after only a few hours at home they toppled over, fell down dead, but still, all he could do was try to persuade the gentleman with no intention whatever of trying to force the issue, so if the old man didn't want to come along, he would just let it be. The old gentleman replied that he'd be more than happy to go with the driver, but that just couldn't be now because of the grandson who was having such a hard time waiting for him, or rather the grandson was having such a hard time waiting for the package of sweets, and he was furthermore of the belief that he had not suffered a concussion, nor did he believe in such a thing as concussions at all, since he was feeling well. The ambulance driver rather peevishly got back behind the wheel and drove off. The old gentleman then thanked you very courteously once more and said good-bye. You then started walking, headed toward the nearby Hernals Beltway, the old gentleman behind you, in his hands the package of sweets wrapped in paper with the name of that bakery on Jörger Strasse on it, wearing a black hat and a black coat, and his pace was very leisurely, wasn't it?

You will perhaps be wondering, dear sir, why I am writing all this to you, but the older gentleman in question is none other than my own father. Having arrived at home, he immediately told me at that time—and continues to do so to the present day, with great agitation, all about his dangerous experience, as you will have already taken to cognizance from this letter, and practically every day he tells me anew all about that Saturday afternoon, with a view toward possibly tracing out such further deliberations about this instructive event as have not yet come to his awareness. As his son I would like to express to you, dear sir, my great thanks for the humane solicitude you displayed toward my father, all the more inasmuch as my father is governed by the conviction that had you not brought such effort to bear in offering him an explanation with such great conscientiousness at just this point in his life, he might well never again have been able, from that time up to the present day, that is, to regain his bearings.

It goes without saying that he wishes to convey his highest thanks to you once again, and he apologizes that he is unable to write to you himself because of his poor eyesight, for which reason he has charged me, as his legally authorized representative holding full power of attorney, to assure you herewith, by this means, and to the most extensive possible degree of particularity, of his profound sense of appreciation for the service you rendered him, whence he also has charged me to inquire if he might permit himself, should such a thing fall within the range of what your valuable time permits, to request that you visit that bakery on Jörger Strasse from time to time, preferably, perhaps, every Saturday afternoon at the same time, for the purpose of being able further to discuss with you to its logical conclusion the above-mentioned set of circumstances, including any and all such effects, outcomes, and consequences as might yesterday, today, and on into distant future days have eventuated from it, but in addition to invite you now and again in the course of those meetings to be his guest for a jelly doughnut. With cordial salutations and expressions of the highest esteem.

P.S. Is it not altogether possible that the course of our life in its entirety is determined by nothing other than an unremitting and regrettable or even lamentable captivity founded on a curious aggregation of altogether ceaseless and incredibly unremitting post-hypnotic suggestions?

# DANUBE RIVER BRIDGE

Some years ago I would often walk from bridge to bridge along the banks of the Danube, undecided every time as to the most convenient point for my daily river crossing, first in one direction and then back, during which—it was usually on the bridge then called the "old Reichsbrücke"—I would stand leaning over the rail for a while, looking down at the river's eyes as they drifted past below, and then spitting down into the river before I resumed my crossing. To this day I am absolutely certain that my spitting down into the water from the bridge was in no way connected with its bringing good luck, as a simplistic folk belief would have it, but was rather a kind of substitute for my not spitting my bodily self in its entirety over the railing along the firmament. Instead of a complete plunge into the river, then, I let drift downward just a few words or sentences, now rendered unutterable through liquefaction, dissolved in my oral cavity from keeping silent so long, as a form of *pars pro toto*, representing on the whole the whole of me there on the back of the river, all the way to the Black Sea, and perhaps being given thereby the opportunity to become better acquainted with somewhat more of what's called the wide world than the torso which was the remainder of my existence, stuck fast here owing to its lethargy and the weight of its body—or something like that. On this one particular morning, very early, no later than five A.M.—incapable of any acceptable activity, I had been stumbling my way through quite a few days and restlessly wandering with no aim for many sleepless nights; why is a different story that doesn't belong here—I was roving around the area by the Danube, as usual, and wanted to conclude by initiating what had grown to be my traditional crossing, which struck me, whenever I started out, incidentally, and on the way back too, as a kind of international border crossing, except this time—and I'm absolutely certain of it to this day—I wasn't going to spit *pars pro toto* into the river but was finally, no matter what, in my entirety, going to drop downward into the river, among its numberless gray eye threads tied together by water, meaning that this time there would have been a one-way international crossing only.

When I drew near the foot of the bridge, however, I saw that a rather large crowd of people had assembled there. That wasn't at all to my liking, and no sooner was I beginning to make a path for myself through this five-A.M., dawn's-early-light gathering of Viennese than I found out from what people were saying that the Reichsbrücke, up onto which I had just now been wanting to walk so as, on this very day, to take a plunge into the river, downstream to the Black Sea—the Reichsbrücke, as I found out from the people's chatter, had collapsed only a few minutes before, buckling and plummeting into the river. That was quite a shock. Less for the crowd happily gaping at the break of dawn, always enthralled anew, as though for the first time, by any disaster that happens their way, than for me, who naturally saw myself as cheated, triple-crossed—my plans crossed out, crossed through, crossed over by this bridge—and simply made a fool of. At the very least, I felt it to be an outrageous impertinence. Here I am, ready to plunge from the bridge into the Danube and onward to the Black Sea, when—right in front of my face, before I even have a decent chance to put my plan into practise—the Reichsbrücke itself takes a plunge into the Danube instead, right smack down into the stream coursing its way to the Black Sea beaches, without, incidentally (and thank God, too!), as I was able to find out from the happily excited murmurings of the early-dawn palaver among these Viennese foregathered so early, without any injuries—not a single soul got it this time—because there happened to be nobody on the bridge at this early hour.

The bridge from which Robert Schumann, whose life and music I was just at that time studying on an altogether scholarly level—at least as intensively as my inner state permitted—the bridge from which he went plunging into the Rhine still spans its river in Düsseldorf today, by the way, the same as always, but the bridge from which I wanted to plunge into the river went and spoiled it by taking a plunge of its own immediately before I could take mine, simply locked me out, took off just as I was getting there, ran away from me at a mad dash, at the last minute, head over heels, wanted absolutely nothing to do with me, and so I am absolutely certain still today that if, on that early morning back then, I had not resolved to throw myself off the Reichsbrücke into the Danube but had intended instead just to spit down into the river from its midpoint, as I always had, it would never have taken its own plunge on that early morning at around five A.M. but would still be standing there unchanged, in its old form, to this very day. Which is how it is that at bottom I'm the person in fact responsible for its collapse, but of course no one ever thought such a thing at the time, and I'll continue to be careful, today and tomorrow, not to wave it in anybody's face; people needn't think I'm that stupid.

## CARYATIDS AND ATLANTES—VIENNA'S FIRST GUEST WORKERS

In the morning, the city of Vienna is usually shrouded in a low-lying cloud, out of which it slowly unwraps itself with great exertion and, varying in accordance with what demands the day is presenting, mounts nine to fifteen feet, or even as high as twenty-one to twenty-seven feet, up the stairwell of the arena in the air, up into the lofty forenoon.

By midday this dignified posture has grown too uncomfortable, which is why, well before then, Vienna will furtively have subsided to its customary level so as to settle back into the cozy afternoon, throughout which you can put up with anything until well into the evening, whose gray fur blanket the city pulls up over its ears before slowly submerging several yards, crumbling through the moth-eaten outer skin of a lowland full of holes, as though the buildings were being sucked under such that only the pointy nightcaps of a few smokestacks are still sticking out, the helplessly fluttering outspread wings of a few roofs unsteadily sailing over the springtide floods that cut furrows as they set in at twilight, murmuring at the edge of hearing, glimmering all the while, before the city slips beyond the eye of the beholder.

In the morning, the walls discharge out of their windows the bedroom linen from overnight; the roof beams cough out of asthmatic chimneys; many buildings sneeze from their open skylights; now and then an entrance gate will push out onto the street a stairwell burst loose from all its flights of steps; sometimes, too, whole suites of rooms are thrust right out through the wall onto the public squares, while cellar vaults are pushing back down their heaps of potatoes, rebelliously bobbing up, as numberless blobs of smoky mist from bulging coal sacks now exploded with a pop are being blown toward the grating over the windows and out into the bustle of the traffic on the street.

On more than a few days, the buildings pull in the protruding bellies of their corbeled bay windows, bashfully fold back their elegantly tapering balustrades, as though they were obeying a command to assume the rigid, straight-wall stance of a surface flattened all smooth by a trowel.

On more than a few days, the streetcar tracks jump up out of the asphalt, shake off the stops that annoy them, and move the last stop a few feet up into the air.

It was then that I really made the acquaintance of those remarkably different creatures in Vienna. By then, I had been holding intense conversations with them for a long time, immersing myself more and more thoroughly in them, so that I might fathom the forms of their existence, forms I was attempting to understand precisely, along with the world in which they dwelt in a way clearly inscrutable to me and in which they were also unquestionably mobile, even though *apparently stationary.*

But how had it all begun? Had I just come to a stop and yelled over to them, Hey! Hey, you there!?

No. That would have struck me as not only tactless, but intrusive as well. Instead, I once felt myself suddenly being accosted from behind, but on turning around, I saw nothing. Only a look shot my way from the rigid face of a stone woman, a caryatid, whose hands were holding the balcony of a building hoisted toward the sky in such a way that she could have hurled it at any time. I knew perfectly well that it could only have been she who called out to me so threateningly, and I was preparing to reply in the same tone of voice, to say I wouldn't tolerate being spoken to like that, and to demand an apology, when I began to think or sense that a whole assembly gathered round about me under gateways, protruding windows, balconies, and other such decorative accoutrements all along the façade of the building was barring my path and, with a marble quivering that set in gently, was beginning to laugh at me. When I inquired as to the reason for their derision, to all appearances directed my way, the reply was: Oh no, this wasn't derision but delight, as well as gratification that there was once again, after only a few decades, a person who understood enough to have an inkling of what they were talking about, what their occupations consisted of, how they passed their days, their wall season calendar schedules on the building-front epochs, and so on—what a happy coincidence, whereupon the decision was made that we would meet every day.

Yes, all of you please come to my apartment right away, to-morrow, I at once joyfully proposed to the caryatids and atlantes (which is what their men are called), of course they were cordially invited to my place at any time, I would in future expect the fullest possible contingent of them to show up at my door whenever they pleased, and a visit from the telamones (which is what they are collectively called), welcome at all times of day or night, would cheerfully brighten the twilight solitude of my quiet rooms!

Unfortunately, however, not a single opportunity arose for me to regale them with the food and drink of my frugal, hospitable seclusion, for they naturally never came to my apartment, because that would have been too cumbersome in various respects, above all much too prolonged.

Even so, I looked them up regularly, questioned them about the nature and condition of their world, and their view of the world, and their concept of existence, as well, of course, about their walled-in daily lives.

How did we manage to communicate?

Whereas I spoke as slowly as I possibly could, pausing whenever possible between words and syllables at intervals of several seconds, only by which means everything I stated or asked would pass into their hearing or understanding, even when I was speaking softly or was often, for that matter, merely thinking; they, on the other hand, shaped their utterances in the form of a "glittering vibrancy" about the nearby space, aided by the light enveloping them, whereupon it seemed to me that I was "hearing" something, or at any rate understanding by means of my senses, for "hearing" is probably not the right word for whatever it was, inasmuch as when I would listen to the telamones, it frequently felt to me *as if I were hearing with my eyes.*

The telamones lived, as I then soon found out, in a world—of course neither comprehensible nor visible at first—marked by a condition in which movement proceeded with infinite slowness and all the forms and formulas of their existence appeared to be characterized by virtual standstill. Making a fist with one of their marble arms, for instance, and then bringing that stone fist down onto the head of a fleeting passer-by, or using the back of their concrete hand to send sprawling with a ruthlessly forceful shove some speed demon of a female bucking the foot traffic, or ripping the seat out of the pants of some disrespectful slob relieving himself at the feet of their solitary evenings and nights would often have required, depending on their location and their stance, two to three years, but possibly also twenty or thirty, and even in extreme cases two or three centuries.

This infinitely slow course of their days and years was in no way paralyzing; rather, it was a prerequisite for their existence and a way of protecting them. What was *air* to them, as I attempted to explain and compare to myself, air which I not only breathed but which constituted the space I occupied within the earth's atmosphere, was to the telamones the incalculably enormous *time* they had available to them, *time* they apprehended as a physically concrete entity. Indeed, they required eternity-dimensional masses of time clouds all around them, which they then somehow "breathed," although "breathed" was again the wrong word, of course. In order for us to be able to imagine all this more clearly, we can agree that these beings did not inhale and exhale normal air, as we do, but required instead a kind of "time gas" or a certain mixture of "time gas" for breathing.

They had no objection to my sharing my time with them, though it was ridiculously brief by telamonic standards of measurement.

Not long after that I had once again been spending several uninterrupted days and nights with them, and another evening had advanced very far, when my eyes fell shut, and so it was that I passed that night, and deep into the following day, if not the evening—or perhaps even longer; I don't know anymore—lying sheltered in their stone shadows, in the marble drapery of the rear courtyards made by their backs.

When I woke up, they were in an extreme state of helpless agitation about me and what they at first surmised was my *sickness*, from which I had supposedly now recovered; several of them had in fact almost given up on me as having passed into an immobile, crumbling death by timelessness, assuming I had collapsed in on myself and turned into the rubble of a death—unambiguously puzzling to them—caused by forfeiture of time.

At any rate, they had been duly afraid for me, had feared I might continue just lying there like that and simply diffuse myself, as patches of cloudily vaporized air, into the ambient evening, whereas I had now finally gotten back up.

I slept only a little, I then said, had been very tired, not to say more exhausted than I had been for a long time. What was it, though, that had struck them all as so especially unusual; what was it about me—or possibly against me—all of a sudden?

Sleep? Tired? What did I mean?

I had fallen into a deep sleep, I told them, and tried to stipulate for them the extent to which it had reinvigorated me.

Sleep?! But what was that and why and what for and how and where did it come from and where might it lead?

What I wanted to do next was give them at least some idea of my dreams, though I had already forgotten them, but they didn't understand. Dreams—what do you mean? they kept asking, until I finally realized that up to this point of their existence the telamones had never heard of sleep, of being sleepy, sleeping dreamers, since until now tiredness or weariness in any form had been entirely unfamiliar to them.

No, they had never known until then what sleep is, what it's good for, to whom or what it is of service; and how, for that matter, were they supposed to have had even the remotest knowledge of any such thing, since no provision had ever been made on their behalf for even a hint of anything in the nature of sleep, because the slightest trace of telamonic fatigue would have caused half the buildings in the city to go weak in the knees and cave in, giving way by night, during a marble sleep, in the disconsolateness of dream-disaster mountains of debris and rubble made of the collapsed walls of the burned-out buildings of submerged cities from carelessly forgotten wars; indeed, it would have been exactly like a war, a *telamonic sleep war* against the city.

Even the *word* "sleep" was unknown to them at the time; they had no equivalent at all in their language.

They had never yet been tired, been weary, trapped instead in petrified wakefulness, walled in by the need for a sleeplessness that had stood the test of timelessness. That was why it was initially such a great effort to furnish them with explanations they could comprehend. I began with just the word "sleep," elucidating over and over again for weeks what it signified, represented, designated, so as to help them lovingly apprehend it, as well as all the phenomena related to it, with complete accuracy of detail, so as to provide them with at least a provisional basis of understanding or insight.

Soon the telamones were so fascinated by a phenomenon altogether new and mysterious to them that they demanded to know more and more about it, because little by little sleep struck them as offering a potential opportunity, opened up to them all of a sudden, for a new and wide-ranging form of art, the amazement connected with their great admiration for which they could not refrain from manifesting.

Yes, it was a wonderful time of my life then, perhaps one of the most wonderful ever; under the tutelage of my highly valued expertise, caryatids and atlantes from almost the whole city started off with my theoretically meticulous *research findings on the fundamentals of sleep*, and the comprehensive *sleep lectures*, as well as the *dream seminars* connected with them, all of which I held, with no intermission, as chair of their petrified gatherings—the content being the entire set of phenomenologies associated with this area of research, such as *half-sleep, deep sleep, noontime sleep, daydreams, the dream-night or, along the same line, the time frame of sleep before and after midnight*—enjoyed great popularity and the best of success, and their eagerness for knowledge of everything connected with this topic, along with their attendant *wakefulness*, displayed in the way they polished off the days and nights that followed, was simply immense.

Soon thereafter the telamones approached me with an especially heartfelt request to move to the practical part of the exercises, beseeching me *for my sleep*, exhorting me to give them an actual demonstration—with absolute clarity, as often as I possibly could, and with utmost thoroughness—of sleep, *from the twilight of dropping off to the first gray dawn of waking*, along with every potentially concomitant circumstance, thereby proceeding from theory to practise, as already noted.

Thus began the most restful and most unconscious period of my life, when all I would do was *sleep practically all the time*, because the telamones couldn't get enough of observing my sleeping form and the dance presentations of my dreams.

My sleep performances soon came to be esteemed as a wondrously exotic, serenity-inducing form of *Gesamtkunstwerk* or all-encompassing work of art matchlessly flung high aloft by me, in all its incalculable vastness, into the air of those day-nights and night-days, aided by the sheer force of my individual personality.

That was why my body was passed along the line from building to building, with as few gaps as possible, from caryatid to atlas (the masculine singular), for the purpose of disseminating my *sleep concerts, slumber plays, dreamer serenades, fatigue tragedies, exhaustion comedies*, all to be marveled at, with feelings running ever higher, as the ultimate or penultimate secret lighting up for them the transfiguring significance of their immobile existence, to the point of a mysterious dissolution of their universal formula for the petrifaction equation.

It's almost unnecessary to mention that many of them were also attempting to penetrate to the ultimate dream depths, which to them were soaring unfathomably high up, for the related purpose, at first formed in secret, of learning sleep itself.

But for nought. None of them came anywhere near doing so; and how would they? As if I, on the other hand, had attempted breathing their "time gas" instead of air!

Nonetheless, or perhaps for that very reason, my snoring presentations, dedicated to a breathlessness on their part enduring for centuries, were more and more in demand; no sooner would I wake up than I would immediately be booked for a new engagement to conduct one of my sleep demonstrations.

As a result, I drank more and more alcohol and took stronger and stronger sleeping pills and liquids, because naturally it's impossible *to sleep honestly* almost all the time without faking it, all the more within the format of artistic demonstrations carried out before the public, the very kind I was holding in my new capacity of, on the one hand, *a creative sleep artist* who had come to wide notice and had even attained fame among them, and, on the other, *a sleep interpreter engaged with the completed creation.* To lie to them by pretending to sleep during my appearances without really sleeping was something I simply could not do to them or expect them to accept, first because they didn't deserve such dilettantism and second because they would have unmasked at the very outset any such efforts to deceive, inasmuch as they had pursued their groundwork in theoretical knowledge with such grim determination that it was no longer possible to fool them.

Every time one of my presentations was well under way, the stone women would first carefully raise those faded curtains, the lids of my eyes, so as to measure by the position of my pupils the intensity of my sleep at this initial stage; they would then move into slowly rocking my outstretched form, slack as a sack, to and fro, loosely, languidly, lightly, and swinging it back and forth so as to determine whether the depth of my sleep was satisfactory; then they would begin giving the sandbag of my body a very sound shaking, hurling it all the way up to the cloud ruins of the weather stadium and then catching it; as a finale, they would slowly, carefully fling me up, up, and away over the gables of even the highest rooftops, tossing to one another the squashed, crumpled package of my body.

None of which did anything to alter the inexorable course of my physical deterioration, owing primarily to the necessary increase in dosage of the soporifics I required for the continuation of my work of not just presenting but also of intensifying the quality of my unconsciousness in the service of sleep scholarship, because, of course, the demands of my immured female devotees and of my male admirers made of stone were increasing as well, until I one day—or one night—reached a point beyond which I could not go on, in that no sleeping potion could help any longer and my terrible state turned out to be a petrifying *torture of wakefulness* for me, so that I was unfortunately compelled on the grounds of sickness to withdraw from a world of telamones grown very dear to me, from their sleep-theater palaces, after I had postponed till indefinite further notice all performances scheduled for the immediate future, now to pass without me, for the sole purpose of learning to give up drinking alcohol and taking sleep-inducing pharmaceuticals.

Once recovered from the stresses and strains of my sleep demonstrations, the first thing I wanted to do was go right back to the caryatids. But when I arrived at the stone walls along which I had made the acquaintance of the stone women, I at once experienced a bitter disappointment: during my absence, the building had either been torn down, owing to an imminent threat of collapse, or it had come tumbling down on its own, an alternative I kept hearing with some reluctance; more exact information was hard to come by.

Should I not have given those who were at that time my best friends, male and female, credit for exercising the deepest sense of purpose in *causing* the building to collapse by abruptly stepping away one night from their places along the façade? Had I not heard them several times voicing sentiments more or less to the effect that they were finding this building and everything it sheltered an ever more unsustainable burden, and did that not become even more clear to me in that there were found within the piles of rubble and ruins, as I was soon easily able to discover, documents containing such informational reports by the secret police as had been made public?

Could they possibly have learned sleep after all in my absence? Had they grown weary, darkness-petrifaction-drowsily drawn down inward toward the center of the earth as the opening of the trap doors in the vast planetary network of cellars commenced?

But wasn't I better off, on the other hand, not having any more encounters with these women of stone?

Possibly I might otherwise not have withstood sore temptation, would have gone back to them immediately, which meant that matters would inevitably have been bound to take their course all over again, new but yet similar to the course already described, along with a similar ending, because every stage would have had to be gone through again, in exactly or almost exactly the same way, with nothing omitted, only to arrive once more back at this very point, one that had indeed been reached now, albeit with effort.

Or might I perhaps have been altogether incapable of reaching this present point a second time, inasmuch as the magnitude of a disaster possibly hurtling toward me right now, even while successfully lurking in ambush for the moment, might have revealed alarming dimensions, ones not needing to be entered into in detail here?

I was fervently devoted to these calcified memories and vividly present to them for a long time.

That manifested itself in particular along the lines of a most distinct and characteristic feeling, to which I was subject with decreasing frequency; it was that I was making myself out to be a very mobile caryatid, or rather, a very lively atlas, admittedly not having to support or bear up a house, a gateway, or a bow window on his shoulders, but in place of burdens like those, however, I bore one the weight of which was assuredly not to be underestimated by comparison, one whose uttermost scale was unimaginably overwhelming to me, one accompanying me faithfully in all my comings and goings: a column of air that reached from my shoulders all the way up to the final, outermost membrane of the atmosphere's roofbeams, a burden that had recently been growing ever more wearisome to me. I can't do this much longer, I often thought, when I would be gasping for breath during attacks of weakness accompanied by nausea, no, I thought to myself, not me, I just can't! And I would often attempt to shake off this column of air. But there was no shaking it off; it stuck to me as doggedly as if it were part of me.

Sometimes I would meet with success after all, though, but it took me a long time to figure out how: from a position of repose, say outside somewhere, sitting on a park bench and starting with some time of focused unwinding; then simply resting and closing my eyes, with my body, and above all my head, balanced in complete equilibrium; then I would notice how my inner state of relaxation would pour out from inside, pour out into the column of air, until I could very distinctly sense that the cylinder of atmosphere on my shoulders was beginning to feel fluffy or fleecy and was twirling or bobbing up and down with something approaching elegance, often shimmering with iridescence as it did so, shifting back and forth on my shoulders as if on two gigantic wings of incalculably vast expanse tightly knotted out of some densely woven fabric made of different threads of crystal; then all I would have to do was wait until the column of air had come completely to rest and fallen asleep; at that point it was really easy to slip it off, but that usually resulted in its waking up at once and hopping straight back up onto my shoulders and perching there. For that reason I would have to dash off instantly, as fast as I could, the split second I had shed the column of air, just take off sprinting to anywhere. But that didn't help for very long either because shortly after coming to rest so as to savor my new-found relief, here came the column of air to take its place again on my head and shoulders; it was the same old one again, having run after me; it had pursued me and always would pursue me, had sought me out and found me again; or it was a different one, a new column of air that had finally found itself a free shoulder; that seemed more logical to me, in fact, and sometimes I would see throughout the whole ambient atmosphere the pushing and shoving of iridescent columns of air, fighting one another as they wandered aimlessly, all the while keeping a lookout for an empty shoulder on which to perch, or rather pounce.

These moments of liberation, extremely brief as they only too often were, made me very happy nonetheless, so that I continued to find these attempts to run away rewarding and hence carried out with ever-greater frequency the measures already described.

The one stupid thing about it was that any people observing me as I would suddenly break into a run not only grew suspicious of me at once in a general way but were utterly certain I had robbed them of something or done something awful to them, something criminal, because I would immediately hear them hysterically calling after me, Stop him! Criminal! Stop that murderer! and more of the same. One time, when I actually was detained by the forces of law and order and, in reply to questions about the reasons for my being so noticeably in a rush, told them about the column of air, I of course was not believed. But because they didn't find any stolen goods on me, they let me go on my way.

Oftentimes, passing by caryatids or atlantes, I would stop and spend some time in their midst, not establishing contact, to be sure, though very often intending to propose to one or another of them that he or she should take some time away for a change as a way of relaxing a little, should stop by a coffeehouse to read the newspapers or a movie house to see one of the films being recommended, because during the time of their absence I would make myself available to support the entrance gate temporarily or to hold the balcony up toward the sky, and to any objection as to my being no doubt too weak for the job, I would have had my counterargument instantly at the ready: if I had been dealing with my column of air all this time, then surely I would be capable of hoisting such little things as houses and gateways for some while.

Every time I would finally decide to launch into my speech on the subject, however, it occurred to me that I would unfortunately have too little time. Centuries for just a small coffee, or millenia just to watch the weekly newsreel—no, that much time I unfortunately did not have.

It was important, even so, and getting to be high time for not only me, but for everybody else in Vienna as well, to start showing a little more respect to the telamones than they had before. It was to be feared that they might otherwise grow sick and tired of continuing to support so many buildings in Vienna.

Well, what if they just fell asleep one day, on purpose, I mean? Half of Vienna would collapse, which would then be like an undeclared war breaking out—or breaking down.

Had these beings made of stone not already, in a way ever more accessible to general comprehension, begun raising their voices at pedestrians walking past, hurling stone curses at their backs? People were surprised, of course, when they were railed at in such an unseemly way right in front of their own houses and, when it first started, would even shake their heads at such behavior, gone completely off the rails, but, as with so many other things, they soon grew used to it. More and more often, however, these volleys of masonry swearing were connected with unpleasant physical pains. The pedestrians walking past the rows of buildings often remained standing as though frozen or rooted to the spot, pausing as though they had felt a painful blow from some projectile whizzing through the air to the back of their head or to their back itself. But no trace was to be seen of either the marksmen or the remains of stones or any of the other projectiles about which there was so much speculation.

They were petrified words. Oh yes, it was ever more obvious that the telamones had begun putting up a fight against the people in the city. And that was exactly as it should be.

At least as far as appearances went, though, there was a real fear that they wouldn't be able to hold up for very much longer; often, in fact, the walls took to shouting incessantly and indiscriminately, in ways fit to crumble the whitewash and set up a cloud of mortar dust, at everyone who happened to be passing by! And even in case they didn't have the capacity to learn sleep, I thought, they would sooner or later—perhaps very slowly but no less surprisingly for that—walk away from the buildings and leave a city turning to rubble and ashes behind them, out to the plains by the shore of the sea, on a journey to the coastal cliffs of the ocean, to the quarries out of which they had been hewn.

It had been a long time by now since my breaking off contact with the telamones, but then again it seemed so short to me, as if that day had been only yesterday on which I walked by a caryatid located not so very close to the center of the city and, moved somehow, came to a stop in front of her.

Did I want to try establishing contact with them again?

Why was I standing once more before this one caryatid supporting with her gently curved shoulders a protruding tower made of bay windows that ran floor upon floor up the height of the building?

Suddenly I knew why, for I was affected by a look that seized me so deeply I felt pierced through by it.
    When had I last felt a look like that?
    The first time this woman glanced at me, I asked myself what someone with eyes like those might be seeing.
    My presumption was that eyes like those missed nothing; glanced at by them, virtually everything was so moved.
    Yet I in no way felt seen through.
    Had it seemed to me that I in fact *had* been seen through, however, I would gladly have let myself be looked at until entirely transparent!

On the skin of my eyes I could feel exactly how that woman was allowing only a silhouette or outline of her facial contours to waft gently through the light between us and brush past my lashes as a mirrored replicate, to the point where her image grew fixed and lingered on the cells of my iris, as if out of her scarcely clouded eyes pleasant weather had settled in over the open fields of my vision.

It was almost as if I were touching the caryatid across the distance from me to her, as if I could already feel her very deeply without having to cleave the surging stream of air between us, to swim toward the shoreline of her voice so as to gather up some of the flotsam and jetsam of her scarcely begun sentences from the breakers of her glances, trained on me still and now suddenly dropping down over me like a veil. It seemed to me that I was "hearing" something, although "hearing" wasn't the right word; rather, it was an iridescent flutter and shimmer of shadows twinkling through the district.

Listen, I thought I detected the woman of stone saying, Listen!

Yes, I felt myself answering, I'm understanding you.

She had already heard so much about my sleep skills, the caryatid seemed to be adding, as I had exhibited them in the past and as they had been described in stories told to her, only I had neglected up until now to bring any of them out here where she was and show her.

I was sorry, I replied, but at that time I had unfortunately never heard of her; if I had, I could guarantee that I would not have let anything like that happen.

Might I perhaps in this regard soon be finding more time, very much more time indeed for her, she asked, provided it wouldn't entail a terrible amount of bother?

Absolutely, any amount of time.

Would you have more time than usual—almost always?

Oh yes.

Then please come lie down by me as soon as possible, as long as you can, dear one, and go to sleep, sleep the whole time you're with me, whenever you want, and when I'm done studying your sleep after half an eternity, when some day, thanks to the especially vigilant care you take of me—with sleep all around, surrounded by sleep—I really am able to learn sleep, so that I would no longer be restricted merely to observing your sleep but could also begin to sleep with you . . . you understand . . . with one another . . .

I said, Oh yes, I understood. I'd come right back to her as soon as possible so that we could get started.

Beforehand, a few things necessary to our joint venture would have to be obtained.

I live all the way out at the other end of the city, I told her. But I'd be right back.

Just take your time, she called after me, it makes no difference whether you're gone for a little while or a long time; I will always know how to find some way of being by your side, even if I can't come with you. After all, we've somehow always been together all along, never parted more than briefly.

## QUICK ORIENTATION

In Vienna there's an *Earth Mound Square* (*Erdbrust Platz*). It's located in the middle of Ottakring—that's the name of the Sixteenth District—and can be reached by streetcar line J (J as in *Josefstadt,* the Eighth District, through which the J passes), the bend of whose tracks at the last stop wraps around the square like a shirt collar always properly starched, encircling the neck and choking off the windpipe.

There's also a *Heaven Street* (*Himmel Straße*). It doesn't begin, on the other hand, until well past the bend of the tracks at the last stop of the 38 trolley (Schottentor to Grinzing), from which point it leads out of this outlying district, a little wine-growing village purposely aged for idyllic effect, seducing as it goes, while behaving at first in the most mannerly way, a few exceptionally genteel houses typical for this end of the city, haughty as only the pettier aristocracy can be, houses assigned to protect it on its route, soon leading them upward, almost airborne, to the somewhat higher-lying vineyards behind them, only to take them along as it goes pitching and swaying among the hazy, indistinct hillcrests along the bright green waves of meadow surf at the edge of the Vienna Woods, here plunging down, down to the Danube and out past it, outward from the city, pushing on westward, only to slither and slide downward into the land all around a plain opening outward with practically no bounds, all the way—for that matter and in all probability—to the shore line of Lake Bohemia, the northward-leading hiking dunes of which, filled with rustling sounds, allegedly begin far before the Czech border.

# TRANSLATOR'S AFTERWORD

*. . . this ramshackle universe that has nothing
to hold it together but coincidence . . .*
William Faulkner, *The Mansion*

A pile of things flung down at random is
the most beautiful ordering of the cosmos.
Albert Paris Gütersloh, *Sonne und Mond*

A. A violent order is disorder; and / B. A great
disorder is an order. / These two things are one.
Wallace Stevens, "Connoisseur of Chaos"

Artists counter the flux or plain messiness of life through the order of craft. Inside their work, a thing of beauty is a joy forever, and art really is longer than life. But "forever" is only in heaven, while on this mound called earth, flux constantly overthrows order, which is always provisional here below. That is the theme pervading this parody-tribute to the art of autobiography as construct, as a supreme fiction looking backward to trace an order not readily apparent in the haphazard events of our lives. Robert Frost's definition of a poem as a momentary stay against confusion can only give comfort if we downplay the "momentary," with its fair warning that confusion is the default state. The writers quoted above are negotiating between chaos and order, taking on the task of creating order while realizing how card-sharpish is their skill at defying the "ramshackle universe" through beginnings, middles, and ends. Not for no reason did André Gide call his novel about a novelist *The Counterfeiters* or Thomas Mann equate high literary creation with fraud in his *Confessions of Felix Krull, Confidence Man*. Henry James was right—there are no plots in real life.

Yet without order, coherent utterance is impossible. Modernist writers confront the threat of chaos by acknowledging its omnipotence in their artful structures, making the energy of their work the assertion of an order they simultaneously recognize as a ruse. Long before the scientists, writers understood how valid chaos theory is, but they work it out in their own orderly, systematic way.

"The System of Vienna" is Jonke's title, the search for a system informing his journeys from boy to man, from country to city, from idyllic childhood in a garden to battle-scarred maturity, the fiercest battles being with himself on his pilgrim way. The narrator is a mortal precariously balancing between the everlasting lightness of unchanging heaven and the painful upheavals of mutable earth.

Jonke notes in his opening statement of provenance that he composed *The System of Vienna: From Heaven Street to Earth Mound Square* in various forms over decades, beginning in the 1960s with a film called *The System of Vienna*, an early quest for order built around the streetcar network in that city. As in Tennessee Williams's *A Streetcar Named Desire*, the symbolically charged place names of his title are actual last stops on streetcar lines, though Jonke doesn't spoil his invention by disclosing that fact any too soon, leaving it till the end. He was working at a time when writers were erecting in their fiction systems elaborate enough both to articulate complex experiences and to display the effort needed to keep at bay the chaos lurking within those experiences. The systems, no matter what kind, are self-consciously, proudly arbitrary, reminders that the author is a creator, not a copyist. There are the dictionary novels, notably Andreas Okopenko's *Lexikon-Roman* and Milorad Pavić's *Dictionary of the Khazars: A Lexicon Novel*. There are hypertext novels like Geoff Ryman's *253*, the number of passengers in a full subway car in London, whom we can click on in any order if we read the online version, just as we can start the lexicon novels at any entry. There is Georges Perec's *Life A User's Manual*, which takes place in a suspended moment in time and applies to an imaginary 10 x 10 grid superimposed on an apartment building in Paris the problem of moving a knight across a chess board without landing back on the same square. There is Osman Lins's *Avalovara*, organized by the magic square SATOR AREPO TENET OPERA ROTAS, over which a spiral governs movement from letter to letter, character to character, encounter to encounter. All these complicated systems require the inclusion of instructions for use to be built in, but leave it to Jonke to put his last. Right at the beginning, he promises "a few brief words concerning the methodology of the working processes I have adopted" (9), but with typical playfulness he never quite gets around to them, because there isn't any "methodology" anyway—which is not to say there's no pattern.

As much as Jonke is parodying it, that consciousness of arrangement in and of itself, of "working processes," is at the heart of this fiction, too, and his making a game of it only leads to a fuller awareness that system is the literally driving force in *The System of Vienna*.

Jonke's comic approach urges readers at once to embrace and to challenge order in the spirit of Faulkner, Gütersloh, and Stevens. And comedy is needed here, because with a universe inexorably tending to always greater disorder through entropy, any effort to find, articulate, and impose order is and always must be a fool's game. Nature's abhorrence of a vacuum seems part of its abhorrence of unchanging order, as it rushes to fill gaps by dividing, dismantling, and tearing down. In another of Jonke's stories, "the presence of memory," a photographer attempts to recreate in minute detail a garden party he had given exactly a year before, believing that he can nullify time by taking precise replicas at the second party of pictures he had taken at the first. The upshot is an unleashing of chaos on a grand scale, with nature exacting its due by having guests drown in the pond (see Kling 31–32). By definition, entropy provides that the more effort we expend in creating order, the more energy we dissipate, thereby hastening the chaos that will bring an end without even a whimper. Nature always retaliates in Jonke's work when humans try to flout its laws. Mountains tumble, seas rise up, lakes vanish, mutant birds turn murderous and hurtle down from the sky in attack formations, as in *Geometric Regional Novel*. Jonke is the opposite of the Romantic solipsists who believed that things exist only because we thought them into existence. Nature and its workings always thwart our little contrivances.

Who could read Jonke and not recall Sheldon Harnick's "Merry Minuet," popularized by the Kingston Trio around the time of Jonke's earliest work in the mid-1960s? Nature will get us, but "What nature doesn't do to us / Will be done by our fellow man" (Harnick). Totalitarian regimes especially are bound to collapse in utter chaos because our fellow man is trying to impose a rigidity of order that nature disallows. Order indeed makes the trains and streetcars run on time, its momentary triumph a main hallmark of authoritarian and totalitarian regimes gone manic. We cannot adequately assess the unsettling comedies of order and chaos running throughout Jonke's work without calling to mind that he was born in February 1946, a few months after the Nazi defeat, in a country that had at first embraced the new order and then acted like its first victim. It would be hard to picture a writer less politically "engaged" in any standard sense than Jonke, but his whole ambivalent approach to order cannot be read without awareness of Austria's burdened political history. *Geometric Regional Novel* parodies authoritarian bureaucratic regimentation in the form of a six-page-long application to take a walk in the woods, one that must be filled out anew each time, an administrative measure to "protect" the citizenry against unseen, menacing "black men" hiding in the trees. Like Charlie Chaplin in *Modern Times* or Jacques Tati in *Mr. Hulot's Holiday*, Jonke uses comedy to spoof the regimentation of mechanizing and stifling the human spirit.

Like Chaplin, Jonke is sometimes called a satirist, but the critic who dubbed him a "crafty anarchist of language" (Reiterer 90) is more accurate. Satire, chastened by irony, underscores order, while parody, based in excess and exaggeration, unmasks anarchism on its way to chaos. Satire enacts a *reductio ad absurdum*, parody a *multiplicatio ad absurdum*. So the map-guided stroll through "The Small City on the Lake," Klagenfurt, reveals misrule behind the closed doors of orderly shops and businesses as the sentences mimetically grow longer and longer, the vista wider and wider, the correlation of narrative to documentary reality ever more uncertain until the chapter must end in a question mark and a parody of rhapsodic nature writing. So the grandmother's appeal to bureaucracy in "Childhood in the Country" remains ineffective, but a dream takes her from earth to heaven in a parody of magical realism Latin-American style. (Jonke lived for a time in South America and participated in the literary life there.) So the narrator's considered resolve to end his life in "Danube River Bridge" seems to be the one factor needed to set the bridge acting as if on its own. So the narrator finds appreciation, intimacy, and love in a community of statues, as if in a variation on Pygmalion and Galatea, when the statues lose the rigidity of perfect order and take on the living fluidity of disorder, in "Caryatids and Atlantes—Vienna's First Guest Workers." But we may not make it that far, for disorder threatens to kill us even before we are born. The narrator's mother can't find her shoes to go to the hospital; the night watchman, gentler but no less obstructive than the bureaucrats who control access to the woods, doesn't want to break the rules by letting her in though a side door; and when the baby finally enters the world, he's blue. The weft and warp of the cosmos threaten to unravel in muddle that can quickly mount to chaos at any time—*before* birth, itself a trauma.

Jonke balances order and chaos through stylistic strategies as well. Repetition of phrase and clause is a musical device, a technique to create reprises, motifs, or building blocks arranged in different combinations but roughly the same sequence. At their most elaborate, these techniques of repetition enable Jonke to deploy elements of Renaissance polyphony or Baroque canons and fugues, culminating in the "Jörger Strasse Prelude and Hernals Beltway Fugue," with its massive blocks of iteration articulating the whole form. Throughout *The System of Vienna*, sentences that take on more and more subordinate clauses and then subordinations within those subordinate clauses roll forth like mighty Baroque preludes and fugues for organ in the manner of Buxtehude or J. S. Bach, building layer on layer in a complex, gigantic, but lucid structure. It's a commonplace to say that the culture of Austria, like that of Spain—the Habsburgs ruled both for centuries—never experienced a rational Enlightenment and so remains rooted to this day in Catholic and Baroque thinking. Jonke's elaboration bears out that commonplace by showing it to be a precise description of his manneristic style.

Elevating elaboration to an essential value in his Baroque art encourages clauses of such convolution as gradually to slip away from due proportion and begin sprawling over whole pages, gestating storms of thunderwords and getting snarled in syntactic structures no mind could follow, let alone unravel. Jonke's sentences grow out of "asides that have become tangents that have become passages that have become chapters," to quote a character from Jonathan Safran Foer's *Extremely Loud and Incredibly Close* (130), though that might be slightly too tidy and linear a description of Jonke's madcap art. A translator could testify from experience to Jonke's greatness as a parodist of Teutonic bombast, creating clausal monstrosities that postpone the verb for so long that it sometimes never appears, for example. Sentences that purposely get lost, gaps and flaws that actually increase the overall articulation are formal Baroque strategies. Reading Jonke is like looking at the great church of St. Charles Borromeo in Vienna, "the exquisite proportions" of whose "twin belfry towers" Fischer von Erlach could achieve only via "the falseness" inhering in Baroque, "the sham and the emptiness, the imposing facades owing balance and rhythm not to the fulfillment of structural requirements but to the architect's whim: the windows which admit no light, the doorways leading nowhere"

(Crankshaw 167–68). The occasional jettisoning of syntax that seemingly originated in modernist creative procedure turns out to have a lofty historical pedigree, underscoring Jonke's joy in turning Baroque stately mansions into fun houses. On the macro level, harmonious proportions; on the micro, structural zaniness.

Jonke's convoluted structures are clear as music, since music needs to express only its own utterance, unhampered by lexical meaning, but they are bound to grow bewildering as elaborate verbal statements careening through obsessive repetitions. Units that as musical notes reveal "meaning" obscure it as words. Negating this obfuscation in turn, Jonke sets the wild verbal flights to enacting the kind of compulsiveness that develops when people so lack any sense of who they are that they have to concoct a provisional or fantasized identity and then assert it over and over through paranoiac or schizophrenic fictions. The chancellor's assistant who doubts the basic reality of his function in "Furniture Show—Main Promenade in the Prater"; the sculptor who casts the very existence of the scene into question in "Autumn Mist—Rose Hill"; the stamp collector who considers himself a scholar of international repute in "The Stamp Collector in the Vienna Woods"; the fishmonger who imagines he is the most powerful politician in the land in "Wholesale Fish Dealer by the Danube Canal"; the dog owner with a persecution complex in "Attempt to Break out to Klosterneuburg"; and the numbingly repetitive letter writer in "Jörger Strasse Prelude and Hernals Beltway Fugue": these characters fill the horror of their vacuum by incessant jabbering (or scribbling) that creates patterns of infinite regress or endless feedback loops, using language not to explore but to deflect reality, either through delusion or through hyperelaboration that blocks even perception, let alone examination, of their lives.

These characters the speaker encounters are essential before-and-after figures in his autobiography as he moves from being born to finding love. Before the turning point, in all the chapters from "Opera Seminar—Metternich Gasse" through "Wholesale Fish Dealer," these benighted people seriously disconcert him, leaving him confused and sometimes paralyzed. During "In the Course of My Courses—From Neuwaldegg to Schottentor," though, he experiences a flash of insight after which he can face with detachment and poise the crazy dog owner, the vicious neighbors in Hernals, the compulsive letter writer going over and over the episode on Jörger Strasse, and his despondent self, until he has attained the healthy state of finding love—with a statue, but this is Jonke! Note the symmetry: in "Autumn Mist—Rose Hill," the sixth chapter, the speaker is paralyzed, even catatonic, helpless after the doubts raised by the sculptor, while in "Attempt to Break out to Klosterneuburg," the sixth chapter from the end, he remains autonomous and self-motivated, able to walk away from the menace posed by the insane dog owner. Darkness and light play important literal and symbolic roles in each story as well; though it is daylight at the end of "Autumn Mist," the speaker still cannot budge, but he can prudently remove himself in "Attempt," even in the dark hour before dawn.

The nature of the conflict gives *The System of Vienna* its down-the-middle, before-and-after form, and we understand that conflict in turn when we grasp the form. A question of genre needs to be addressed here. *The System of Vienna* is a fantastically fabulated fictional autobiography or an autobiography as exuberantly fanciful fiction, a sequential record of key episodes in the speaker's life.

Adequate terms do not come readily to mind because of the dividing line between fiction and autobiography in English-language literary categories. Joel Agee notes (57), though, that autobiography and fiction are not separate entities in European thought, because both are kinds of narratives constructed with conscious artifice. And because even a strictly factual record of any life cannot be compiled without choosing what to include and omit, autobiography is considered as distinctly belletristic as a "made-up" story. The title of Goethe's autobiography, *Dichtung und Wahrheit* (Fabulation and Truth), bears out the awareness that recording a life demands invention. Skepticism about the accuracy of memory and constant revision of it is the essence of Georges Perec's search in *W or the Memory of Childhood*, and the title of a memoir by Elizabeth McCracken, *An Exact Replica of a Figment of My Imagination*, sums up the inherent, inevitable fabrication any record of experience requires. David Bellos ("Pact of London," Works Cited) discusses the "pact" autobiographers make with readers, promising them some grounding in fact, but it becomes apparent on reflection that the truth content of any autobiography can never be coextensive with its documentary accuracy. William Zinsser titles his anthology of memoirs *Inventing the Truth*—or, to quote a more discursive and less imaginatively charged autobiographical essay by Jonke, "I am an invention of my own self" ("Individuum und Metamorphose" 7).

So there is no contradiction in Jonke's honoring the pact while letting his invention soar. He weaves actual occurrences into an imaginative structure, ensuring a degree of correspondence with events in his life while transmuting them into successive stages of a spiritual journey, shaping a classic pilgrimage narrative complete with a sudden conversion that involves light, loss of orientation, random wandering, and attempts to escape new-found truths. The conversion in *The System of Vienna* is not conventionally religious, but it follows the same process whereby the narrator recognizes in a flash all the fraudulence, pretension, pedantry, and shallowness of his life. William James traces this process in his *Varieties of Religious Experience*, and it is remarkable how closely Jonke's narrator goes from realizing that his is "The Sick Soul" (James 109–38) whose "Divided Self" (139–56) needs "Conversion" (157–59) for him to become who he really is, in contrast to the deluded people accosting him.

Conversion narratives feature almost without exception the pattern just noted. The whole psyche undergoes an instant but total upheaval accompanied by bright light (and sometimes by voices), but the transfiguring vision yields to loss of direction, erratic wandering, and flight until the person assents in a reconstitution of soul that has already occurred. James's sources all document this progression; sudden bursts of light, to give an example of just the onset, are present in every story (169; 175; 179). In *The System of Vienna*, the bored, fed-up narrator is going through his ordinary day at the music department when he suddenly notices "from a window in the corridor on the second floor how the sheen-glinting streetcar tracks, over and past the heat waves of which the multicolored swarms of butterflies aflutter in a summer bursting forth now are skimming . . . " ("In the Course of My Courses" 49) and spontaneously leaves the building, seemingly never to return, after a rapid series of soul-corroding academic encounters, wanders uphill through the city, as if climbing a spiritual mountain, and tries to escape his remade self by running away to Klosterneuburg, only to see enacted there the conflict in his own soul, the contrast between squalor and suspicion and humble fulfillment of one's calling in the person of the man digging the ditch. He is henceforth equipped to negotiate hostility, depression, loneliness, and addiction until he wins through to love, the aim and effect of all conversion.

Lest it appear that some external schema is being forced onto *The System of Vienna*, recall that Jonke's longest discursive autobiographical piece has the pertinent title "Individual and Metamorphosis," emphasizing change as the fundamental need in becoming one's true self, in his case finding his voice as an artist (7–30). In this essay, he presents as life stages variations of the stories in *The System of Vienna*, claiming them equally as factual records (*"Wahrheit"*) and artistic inventions (*"Dichtung"*). Jonke faced in "real" life the same crisis he records here, in which his pretensions to scholarship came to strike him as an "unparalleled swindle," "a fraud on my part against scholarship, which I believed I could attain to, as well as a fraud on the part of the scholarship held against me, which made me believe I was indispensable to it" ("In the Course of My Courses" 49). His subsequent disorientation and period of wandering took the form of his almost drinking himself to death in London, as he told Lux (53) and this writer (Kling Interview). He found himself "faced with a choice either to hang myself or make a change" (Lux 53), and the change, the definitive working out of his metamorphosis, was to give up pointless and self-indulgent "language doodling" (qtd. in Wagner 307), as he saw it, and begin writing on a more subtle and authentic level. The narrator's thoughts of suicide in "Danube River Bridge" and his addiction to sleeping pills in "Caryatids and Atlantes" are fanciful but accurate records of Jonke's "real-life" struggle to work free of alcohol addiction.

*The System of Vienna* documents the problems Jonke faced in his actual life (*"Wahrheit"* again), then, but it does so as art, not reportage, deploying metafictional techniques to remind readers that all writing is fabulation (*"Dichtung"* again), not because art evades or denies truth but because truth can be apprehended in this broken world through the wholeness craft and invention offer. Only through arranging the raw material of life and experience do their patterns emerge into coherence. But we *make* those patterns, for, as Wallace Stevens voices in "Study of Two Pears" (196–97), we can't even begin to see what's "out there" until we model and foreground and order its particulars in our minds. Hence the empowering advice in "The Small City on the Lake" to wrap up the whole square in paper and string, since the square is a figment of writing, not a "real" place. Hence the healthy but bewildering doubt about reality itself expressed by the sculptor in "Autumn Mist—Rose Hill"; he may be conventionally crazy in one way, but he shows how art spins reality out of imagination. The furniture dealers in "Furniture Show—Main Promenade in the Prater" give the speaker a book with the same title, *The System of Vienna*, as the book in which we're reading the story in real time, and the speaker exercises an option open to any reader by throwing it into the trash; this metafictional *mise-en-abîme* humorously varies the situation in Gide's *The Counterfeiters*, in which the main character is a novelist writing a novel called *The Counterfeiters*. "Danube River Bridge" hinges on the relative improbability that a bridge would simply collapse, considerately doing so when no one is crossing it. But that fantasy is actual fact: the Reichsbrücke really did buckle and fall into the Danube at five A.M. on August 1, 1976—a meaningless, random event until the shaping imagination seizes on it. To remind us of how much art is involved in comprehending life, the speaker even reports his own birth as a parody of legend or myth based on oral transmittal, but its hilarious tone of muddle and bureaucratic fuss strategically reverses all the trappings, common to legend and to many an autobiography, of stars and constellations aligned portentously, of signs and wonders, of nature hushed and awed at the birth of this child. After all, what emerges in Jonke is a blue baby, a child almost not viable, marked by mortality even before he starts breathing.

From its title on, *The System of Vienna: From Heaven Street to Earth Mound Square* balances opposites by crafting an order only art can achieve. Heaven and earth; documentation and high artifice; clownishness and spiritual anguish; frustration and fulfillment; *Dichtung* and *Wahrheit*; zaniness and identity crisis—these are all working toward and away from the axis of a conversion narrative. David Foster Wallace, never less than compelling on any subject, might be writing about *The System of Vienna* in some remarks he made about Jonke's fellow Austrian and literary ancestor Franz Kafka, who exhibits ". . . a grotesque, gorgeous, and thoroughly modern complexity . . . a religious humor, but religious in the manner of Kierkegaard and Rilke and the Psalms, a harrowing spirituality." The central joke in Kafka is "that the horrific struggle to establish a human self results in a self whose humanity is inseparable from that horrific struggle. That our endless and impossible journey toward home is in fact our home" (Wallace 64–65). Add a degree of clowning and anarchy not readily apparent in Kafka, and Wallace has given us an apt characterization of Jonke's wildly inventive spiritual autobiography too.

—Vincent Kling

# WORKS CITED

Agee, Joel. "A Lie That Tells the Truth." *Harper's* Nov. 2007: 53–58.

Bartens, Daniela and Paul Pechmann, eds. *Gert Jonke.* Dossier: Die Buchreihe über österreichische Autoren 11. Graz: Droschl, 1996.

Bellos, David. "The Pact of London." www.centerforbookculture. org/casebooks/casebook_london/david.html. 1 Nov. 2008.

Crankshaw, Edward. *Vienna: The Image of a Culture in Decline.* 1938. London: Macmillan, 1976.

Faulkner, William. *The Mansion.* Snopes Trilogy. Vol. 3. New York: Random House, 1959.

Foer, Jonathan Safran. *Extremely Loud and Incredibly Close.* New York: Houghton Mifflin, 2005.

Gütersloh, Albert Paris. *Sonne und Mond: Ein historischer Roman aus der Gegenwart.* Munich: Piper, 1962.

Harnick, Sheldon. "The Merry Minuet." http://www.consciouschoice. com/2006/10/bodymind0610.html. 31 Oct. 2008.

James, William. *The Varieties of Religious Experience: A Study in Human Nature. The Works of William James.* Vol. 15. Ed. Frederick H. urkhardt and Fredson Bowers. Cambridge: Harvard UP, 1985.

Jonke, Gert. *Geometric Regional Novel.* Trans. Johannes R. Vazulik. Chicago: Dalkey Archive, 1994.

———. "Individuum und Metamorphose." *Stoffgewitter.* Salzburg: Residenz, 1996. 7–61.

Kling, Vincent. Gert Jonke. Personal Interview. June and July 2004. Five sessions.

———. "Gert Jonke." *Review of Contemporary Fiction*, 35.1 (Spring 2005): 7–63.

Lins, Osman. *Avalovara.* Trans. Gregory Rabassa. 1980. Chicago: Dalkey Archive, 2002.

Lux, Joachim, ed. *Gert Jonke: Chorphantasie.* (Program Booklet.) Vienna: Burgtheater/Akademietheater, 2003.

McCracken, Elizabeth. *An Exact Replica of a Figment of My Imagination.* Boston: Little Brown, 2008.

Okopenko, Andreas. *Lexikon einer sentimentalen Reise zum Exporteurtreffen in Druden: Roman.* Vienna: Deuticke, 1996.

Pavić, Milorad. *Dictionary of the Khazars: A Lexicon Novel.* Trans. Christina Pribicević-Zorić. New York: Knopf, 1988.

Perec, Georges. *Life A User's Manual.* Trans. David Bellos. Boston: Godine, 1987.

———. *W or the Memory of Childhood.* Trans. David Bellos. Boston: Godine, 1988.

Reiterer, Reinhold. "Listiger Sprach-Anarchist." *Bühne: Österreichs Theater- und Kulturmagazin* May 2003: 90–91.

Ryman, Geoff. *253.* New York: St. Martin's Griffin, 1998.

———. http://www.ryman-novel.com/. 1 Nov. 2008.

Stevens, Wallace. "Connoisseur of Chaos." *The Collected Poems of Wallace Stevens.* 1954. New York: Knopf, 1967. 215–16.

Wagner, Karl. "Gert Jonkes poetische Selbstbehauptung." Bartens and Pechmann. 307–09.

Wallace, David Foster. "Some Remarks on Kafka's Funniness from Which Probably Not Enough Has Been Removed." *Consider the Lobster and Other Essays*. 1999. Boston: Back Bay (Little Brown), 2006. 60–65.

Zinsser, William, ed. *Inventing the Truth: The Art and Craft of Memoir*. Rev. ed. New York: Houghton Mifflin, 1998.

GERT JONKE is the author of *Geometric Regional Novel* and *Homage to Czerny: Studies in Virtuoso Technique*, and is considered one of Austria's most important authors. He received the Ingeborg Bachmann Prize, the Erich Fried Prize, and the Grand Austrian State Prize for Literature, among others. He died in 2009 at the age of 62.

VINCENT KLING is professor of German and comparative literature at La Salle University in Philadelphia.

## SELECTED DALKEY ARCHIVE PAPERBACKS

FOR A FULL LIST OF PUBLICATIONS, VISIT:
www.dalkeyarchive.com

# SELECTED DALKEY ARCHIVE PAPERBACKS

LADISLAV MATEJKA AND KRYSTYNA POMORSKA, EDS.,
  *Readings in Russian Poetics: Formalist and*
  *Structuralist Views.*
HARRY MATHEWS,
  *The Case of the Persevering Maltese: Collected Essays.*
  *Cigarettes.*
  *The Conversions.*
  *The Human Country: New and Collected Stories.*
  *The Journalist.*
  *My Life in CIA.*
  *Singular Pleasures.*
  *The Sinking of the Odradek Stadium.*
  *Tlooth.*
  *20 Lines a Day.*
ROBERT L. MCLAUGHLIN, ED., *Innovations: An Anthology of*
  *Modern & Contemporary Fiction.*
HERMAN MELVILLE, *The Confidence-Man.*
AMANDA MICHALOPOULOU, *I'd Like.*
STEVEN MILLHAUSER, *The Barnum Museum.*
  *In the Penny Arcade.*
RALPH J. MILLS, JR., *Essays on Poetry.*
MOMUS, *The Book of Jokes.*
CHRISTINE MONTALBETTI, *Western.*
OLIVE MOORE, *Spleen.*
NICHOLAS MOSLEY, *Accident.*
  *Assassins.*
  *Catastrophe Practice.*
  *Children of Darkness and Light.*
  *Experience and Religion.*
  *God's Hazard.*
  *The Hesperides Tree.*
  *Hopeful Monsters.*
  *Imago Bird.*
  *Impossible Object.*
  *Inventing God.*
  *Judith.*
  *Look at the Dark.*
  *Natalie Natalia.*
  *Paradoxes of Peace.*
  *Serpent.*
  *Time at War.*
  *The Uses of Slime Mould: Essays of Four Decades.*
WARREN MOTTE,
  *Fables of the Novel: French Fiction since 1990.*
  *Fiction Now: The French Novel in the 21st Century.*
  *Oulipo: A Primer of Potential Literature.*
YVES NAVARRE, *Our Share of Time.*
  *Sweet Tooth.*
DOROTHY NELSON, *In Night's City.*
  *Tar and Feathers.*
WILFRIDO D. NOLLEDO, *But for the Lovers.*
FLANN O'BRIEN, *At Swim-Two-Birds.*
  *At War.*
  *The Best of Myles.*
  *The Dalkey Archive.*
  *Further Cuttings.*
  *The Hard Life.*
  *The Poor Mouth.*
  *The Third Policeman.*
CLAUDE OLLIER, *The Mise-en-Scène.*
PATRIK OUŘEDNÍK, *Europeana.*
FERNANDO DEL PASO, *News from the Empire.*
  *Palinuro of Mexico.*
ROBERT PINGET, *The Inquisitory.*
  *Mahu or The Material.*
  *Trio.*
MANUEL PUIG, *Betrayed by Rita Hayworth.*
  *Heartbreak Tango.*
RAYMOND QUENEAU, *The Last Days.*
  *Odile.*
  *Pierrot Mon Ami.*
  *Saint Glinglin.*
ANN QUIN, *Berg.*
  *Passages.*
  *Three.*
  *Tripticks.*
ISHMAEL REED, *The Free-Lance Pallbearers.*
  *The Last Days of Louisiana Red.*
  *The Plays.*
  *Reckless Eyeballing.*
  *The Terrible Threes.*
  *The Terrible Twos.*
  *Yellow Back Radio Broke-Down.*
JEAN RICARDOU, *Place Names.*
RAINER MARIA RILKE,
  *The Notebooks of Malte Laurids Brigge.*
JULIÁN RÍOS, *Larva: A Midsummer Night's Babel.*
  *Poundemonium.*
AUGUSTO ROA BASTOS, *I the Supreme.*
OLIVIER ROLIN, *Hotel Crystal.*
JACQUES ROUBAUD, *The Form of a City Changes Faster,*
  *Alas, Than the Human Heart.*
  *The Great Fire of London.*
  *Hortense in Exile.*
  *Hortense Is Abducted.*
  *The Loop.*
  *The Plurality of Worlds of Lewis.*
  *The Princess Hoppy.*
  *Some Thing Black.*
LEON S. ROUDIEZ, *French Fiction Revisited.*

VEDRANA RUDAN, *Night.*
STIG SÆTERBAKKEN, *Siamese.*
LYDIE SALVAYRE, *The Company of Ghosts.*
  *Everyday Life.*
  *The Lecture.*
  *Portrait of the Writer as a Domesticated Animal.*
  *The Power of Flies.*
LUIS RAFAEL SÁNCHEZ, *Macho Camacho's Beat.*
SEVERO SARDUY, *Cobra & Maitreya.*
NATHALIE SARRAUTE, *Do You Hear Them?*
  *Martereau.*
  *The Planetarium.*
ARNO SCHMIDT, *Collected Stories.*
  *Nobodaddy's Children.*
CHRISTINE SCHUTT, *Nightwork.*
GAIL SCOTT, *My Paris.*
DAMION SEARLS, *What We Were Doing and*
  *Where We Were Going.*
JUNE AKERS SEESE,
  *Is This What Other Women Feel Too?*
  *What Waiting Really Means.*
BERNARD SHARE, *Inish.*
  *Transit.*
AURELIE SHEEHAN, *Jack Kerouac Is Pregnant.*
VIKTOR SHKLOVSKY, *Knight's Move.*
  *A Sentimental Journey: Memoirs 1917–1922.*
  *Energy of Delusion: A Book on Plot.*
  *Literature and Cinematography.*
  *Theory of Prose.*
  *Third Factory.*
  *Zoo, or Letters Not about Love.*
JOSEF ŠKVORECKÝ, *The Engineer of Human Souls.*
CLAUDE SIMON, *The Invitation.*
GILBERT SORRENTINO, *Aberration of Starlight.*
  *Blue Pastoral.*
  *Crystal Vision.*
  *Imaginative Qualities of Actual Things.*
  *Mulligan Stew.*
  *Pack of Lies.*
  *Red the Fiend.*
  *The Sky Changes.*
  *Something Said.*
  *Splendide-Hôtel.*
  *Steelwork.*
  *Under the Shadow.*
W. M. SPACKMAN, *The Complete Fiction.*
ANDRZEJ STASIUK, *Fado.*
GERTRUDE STEIN, *Lucy Church Amiably.*
  *The Making of Americans.*
  *A Novel of Thank You.*
PIOTR SZEWC, *Annihilation.*
GONÇALO M. TAVARES, *Jerusalem.*
LUCIAN DAN TEODOROVICI, *Our Circus Presents . . .*
STEFAN THEMERSON, *Hobson's Island.*
  *The Mystery of the Sardine.*
  *Tom Harris.*
JEAN-PHILIPPE TOUSSAINT, *The Bathroom.*
  *Camera.*
  *Monsieur.*
  *Running Away.*
  *Television.*
DUMITRU TSEPENEAG, *Pigeon Post.*
  *The Necessary Marriage.*
  *Vain Art of the Fugue.*
ESTHER TUSQUETS, *Stranded.*
DUBRAVKA UGRESIC, *Lend Me Your Character.*
  *Thank You for Not Reading.*
MATI UNT, *Brecht at Night*
  *Diary of a Blood Donor.*
  *Things in the Night.*
ÁLVARO URIBE AND OLIVIA SEARS, EDS.,
  *The Best of Contemporary Mexican Fiction.*
ELOY URROZ, *The Obstacles.*
LUISA VALENZUELA, *He Who Searches.*
PAUL VERHAEGHEN, *Omega Minor.*
MARJA-LIISA VARTIO, *The Parson's Widow.*
BORIS VIAN, *Heartsnatcher.*
ORNELA VORPSI, *The Country Where No One Ever Dies.*
AUSTRYN WAINHOUSE, *Hedyphagetica.*
PAUL WEST, *Words for a Deaf Daughter & Gala.*
CURTIS WHITE, *America's Magic Mountain.*
  *The Idea of Home.*
  *Memories of My Father Watching TV.*
  *Monstrous Possibility: An Invitation to*
  *Literary Politics.*
  *Requiem.*
DIANE WILLIAMS, *Excitability: Selected Stories.*
  *Romancer Erector.*
DOUGLAS WOOLF, *Wall to Wall.*
  *Ya! & John-Juan.*
JAY WRIGHT, *Polynomials and Pollen.*
  *The Presentable Art of Reading Absence.*
PHILIP WYLIE, *Generation of Vipers.*
MARGUERITE YOUNG, *Angel in the Forest.*
  *Miss MacIntosh, My Darling.*
REYOUNG, *Unbabbling.*
ZORAN ŽIVKOVIĆ, *Hidden Camera.*
LOUIS ZUKOFSKY, *Collected Fiction.*
SCOTT ZWIREN, *God Head.*

FOR A FULL LIST OF PUBLICATIONS, VISIT:
www.dalkeyarchive.com